Richard studied Education, Geography and Geology, and graduated from Exeter University in 1977. He entered the field of TEFL, which allowed him to teach abroad in several countries. His love of ornithology started in early childhood, and he used every opportunity to find out more. He worked as a volunteer on a few RSPB reserves and honed his observation skills. He ran ornithology courses at night schools and became the newsletter editor for his county ornithological society.

His notes on migratory birds showed that there has been a shift in their movement due to climate change. He has witnessed the demise of some of the local species: Cirl Bunting, Tree Sparrow and Turtle Dove. There has been a welcome arrival of some Mediterranean species, which is indicative that global warming is causing great changes within the European avifauna.

Iva was born in Czechoslovakia but left her homeland as a young child, in 1969, after the Russian occupation. She resided in West Germany for ten years, where she graduated from high school. On her arrival in England, she became proficient in the language and graduated from Brighton University, in 1992, with an honours degree in Social Policy and Administration. Her natural ability at language acquisition has given her a multitude of skills when it comes to the written word. She loves writing stories and poems, and uses her creativity to the fullest.

To our beloved mothers: Hana and Sylvia,
also to Zdeněk, Babička and Děda.

Richard and Iva Ives

FROM THE BEAKS
OF BIRDS

AUSTIN MACAULEY PUBLISHERS™

LONDON · CAMBRIDGE · NEW YORK · SHARJAH

A CIP catalogue record for this title is available from the British Library.

ISBN 9781788788700 (Paperback)
ISBN 9781788788724 (E-Book)

www.austinmacauley.com

First Published (2019)
Austin Macauley Publishers Ltd
25 Canada Square
Canary Wharf
London
E14 5LQ

Our thanks must go to John Daer, our good friend, who proofread the drafts. We would also like to express our gratitude to the various people who read the book and gave us some useful pointers.

Naturally, we are extremely indebted to Dorian Mason and Linda Favell for providing their beautiful photographs, which have enlivened the text. We are also grateful to Linda for listening to our wishes and providing the powerful 'satanic mills' front cover. My appreciation also goes to all the wonderful people I have met in the field, both here and abroad.

The Photographers

Dorian has managed to capture some wonderful images, as the accompanying photographs show. His work has been published in the local bird reports, magazines and the local press. His website depicts just how proficient he is at taking stunning bird images.

Linda, whom I have known since university, has recently taken up bird photography on her travels. Her excellent portfolio is growing rapidly.

Spring Migration Routes

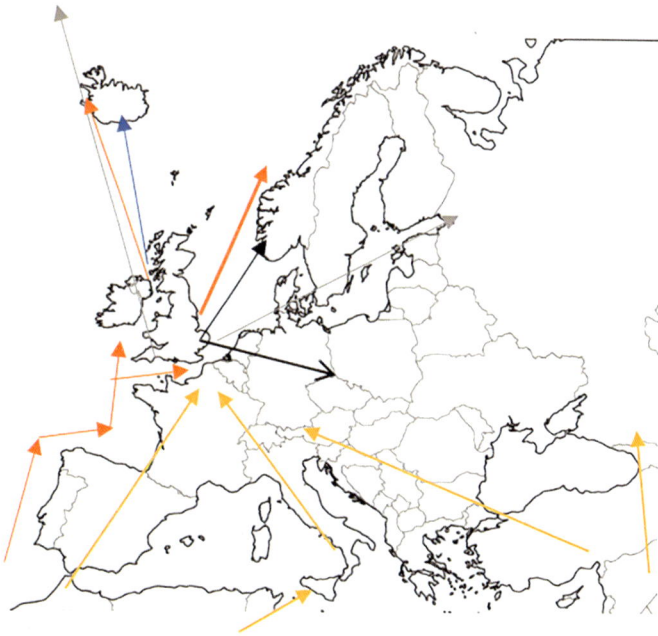

Winter Thrushes	
Bar-tailed Godwit	
Brent Geese	
Terns & Waders	
Swallows, Swifts,	
Warblers, Chats,	
Hobby & Cuckoo	

Most spring migrants will use the narrowest sea crossings hence many fly over the Straits of Gibraltar, or through Sicily and then Italy, or over the Bosporus in Turkey.

In the autumn, the birds travel in the opposite direction.

From the Beaks of Birds

By Richard and Iva Ives

A collection of stories as seen through different eyes

Drawings by Richard Ives
Photographs by Dorian Mason and Linda Favell

Table of Contents

Preface

I have always been inspired by nature, particularly birds, since childhood. As I travelled around the country, I was fascinated by discovering different species in various habitats. Each has an individual story to tell, and we thought it might be interesting to portray their lives in a novel way rather than using a dry, academic approach. Hopefully, we have succeeded in our aim.

If this little book reaches out to anyone and ignites an *active* interest in the natural world, then it will have achieved its objective.

Dipper

Introduction

Off the coast of Europe stands a group of islands famed for its unpredictable weather! The 'warm' seas which lap against the coasts ensure that winters are relatively mild in comparison to the mainland and, as a result, many birds fly here in the autumn to escape the worst of the weather.

The rocks which form these islands have resulted in many different landscapes: the ancient hard rocks to the north and west mean it is mainly mountainous there whilst the younger, softer ones to the south form gentle rolling countryside. The sand and mud washed down from the higher ground often meet the sea and form estuaries which are vital feeding grounds for so many creatures.

These islands were formed when the melting ice from the last ice age formed a barrier between Britain and the rest of Europe. Many creatures, common just across the Channel, are missing as they were too slow to move north before the sea took away their opportunity to find a home here. Therefore, many kinds of plants, insects, frogs, newts, woodpeckers, snakes and even some mammals are lacking.

However, the varied land and seascapes allow a multitude of birds to breed here. The long summer days encourage birds to fly thousands of miles from Africa to utilise the daylight and emerging insects to raise a family.

Here is a collection of some of their stories.

(Words marked with an * can be found in the glossary at the back of the book)

Urban Utterances

Crowded streets, pollution fumes, rows of houses with rubbish
strewn
Not a very inspiring place, yet, in amongst this urban mess
There are numerous birds who here choose to nest
Their dawn chorus clear to hear
Shows that nature is ever near.
Bird tables bedecked with food allow creatures despite their fear
To feast upon this welcome gift to bring cheer
To everyone's day
Just to show that nature is not that far away.

Far away from the wilder places, man had made his mark with his concrete jungles but, even here, life thrives. The spring dawn chorus is surprisingly loud in the middle of suburbia: many birds prosper amongst the well-tended gardens and manicured lawns. Ornamental fruit trees provide a lifeline for Winter Thrushes and even the city centres attract roosting Wagtails eager to enjoy the warmer temperatures that the cities provide.

Two well-fed, somewhat scruffy, Feral Doves, Freya and Phoebe, were sitting in the park soaking up the sun's rays. They usually spend their days picking up scraps from the people who eat their lunches on the park benches.

"Another day in paradise, Freya," said Phoebe ironically.

"Yep. You are right there, my dear," she answered.

"Have you noticed all the changes around?" enquired Phoebe.

"What do you mean?" she asked somewhat perplexed.

"Well, for one thing, I have noticed that a pair of Peregrines and a few Sparrowhawks have moved into the neighbourhood, that's a real worry. The Peregrines love the tall buildings and, to add insult to injury, some idiots have even put up nest boxes to encourage them! What about us? Some people have no consideration. That means we shall have to watch our step in future. They are sublime hunters, and it really puts me off my sandwiches!" said Phoebe nervously.

Sparrowhawk

"Yes. You are right. I hear Mrs Jones' son disappeared last week, and many believe he was served as dinner in the Peregrine household. I really do not know what this world is coming to!" said Freya despondently.

"Well, it seems life is good here in the city. There are so many more birds than there used to be. Have you heard the racket in the morning? Blackbirds, Thrushes, Robins, and Herring Gulls all making such a noise at some unearthly hour! I am sure it wasn't like that in the old days." Phoebe reflected.

"You are absolutely right. Talking about a racket, have you noticed those damn green parakeets? Boy, do they screech!

Rose-ringed Parakeet

"Never heard such a noise! I hear in the west of London there are hundreds roosting in the parks. They seem to find this country's urban life to their liking. Heaven knows where they came from. I am pleased we are here in the city centre where it's 'peaceful'." Freya didn't realise the absurdity of her statement.

"I think things have got much better for other birds, you know. People seemed to have cottoned onto the fact that birds are quite entertaining and so many gardens are full of goodies: peanuts, seeds, suet and, of course, there are more bird baths to keep my plumage in perfect condition." Phoebe glowed.

"Have you ever looked at yourself, my dear?" giving her a knowing look. "I think this urban life has made us a bit scruffy. I am sure our ancestors, the Rock Dove, looked a lot smarter than we do!"

"Hmmm, you may have a point there. Anyway, as I was saying, it seems that people are finally becoming aware that wildlife is an important factor in their life and, as a result, are taking active steps to encourage us into their gardens. Well, when I say 'us', I am not so sure they want feral Pigeons! They have erected bird tables which we really cannot land on and those annoying peanut feeders are a devil to access!" Phoebe said in an exasperated voice.

"Have you noticed those vast flocks of Starlings? They arrive en masse into a garden and wolf down everything on the bird tables. Once that's gone, they then work hard on people's lawns. They seem to be very successful at finding leatherjackets* which means those dreadful daddy long legs are not so common in the autumn, thank goodness, as they make me shudder." Freya sighed.

"You are right there, my dear. I think many are willing to have their bird tables rifled* by Starlings for the benefits they bring to the gardener. Perhaps the bird tables and nut holders are there to deter us rather than encourage us! I think people prefer the little songsters. I have noticed that the Swifts have returned to the city centres since they began to clean up the air a bit. However, it seems that many roof renovations are too good for the poor old Swift, as they can no longer access the loft spaces they need. I see some special nest boxes have been erected for them so perhaps people have realised their plight and are doing something about it." Phoebe announced.

"You were talking about bird baths a moment ago, have you seen how many garden ponds are appearing? I have noticed a lot of dragonflies and damselflies on my travels; it seems that they like their new-found homes. Who would have thought it, having such creatures living in the middle of town?"

"You are absolutely right Freya. There are even newts, frogs and toads wandering around people's gardens. Just unbelievable!"

"Mind you, there are some problems with all this free food and water." Freya added.

"Really? What could possibly be wrong with that?"

"I have spoken to a few poorly birds. It seems they have caught something from the feeders. People forget that they should clean them from time to time as mouldy peanuts are actually poisonous. I wish people knew that, as it is terribly sad seeing a sickly Blue Tit or Greenfinch."

"Absolutely! I wonder if people also know they should clean out the nest boxes after the birds have fledged. There are a lot of nasties in the nest such as ticks and lice. If they are not disturbed over the winter, they lie in wait for the following year to live off the new tenants. These little birds have enough to cope with by having to raise a large family, let alone being plagued by those nasty insects. The poor old Swifts can't really be helped by kind people as their nests are usually inaccessible in people's loft spaces, so the nasties cannot be eradicated. I know that many Swifts carry around ticks for thousands of miles each year! They must be the world's farthest travelling parasites; mind you, they do get to see the world!" Phoebe added.

"Talking of poorly, I met a hedgehog the other day; he really wasn't good. He told me he was thirsty and drank some milk which someone had left out for him. I thought everybody knew that milk is bad for hedgehogs. He also told me he had had a blowout on mealworms some well-meaning person had left in a saucer and they, alone, are not good: it's like eating chocolate all day without anything else! Boy, was he suffering. I hope he finds some more natural food, so he can recover." Freya said hopefully.

"That's a terrible story but mind you, we have our own problems with pesky cats, but then again, have you noticed how many foxes there are here nowadays? They are everywhere! How many times have I been woken up by a dustbin being knocked over by a fox in the middle of the night! Some have no consideration for others; I really need my beauty sleep." Phoebe commented.

"It doesn't seem to have had the desired effect! But you are right, foxes are doing really well. I was in a garden the other day, it was surrounded by evergreens and I was surprised to hear both Goldcrests and Coal Tits singing away. It seems that these birds are moving into town as these new habitats are produced. Good luck to them, I say."

"I concur. The urban environment has really been enriched these last few years. It's a great sign that things are moving in the right direction. I have also noticed that many schools have a 'nature corner' in their grounds, and I often pop in to have a snack from time to time. Very useful, I can tell you."

An urban Peregrine with prey

"Look! There's someone snacking, perhaps we should fly over there and scrounge our first meal of the day."

"Great idea. Let's go!"

The River and an Unusual Visitor

The roaring stream with eddies and falls
Provides a special bird with a home
A small, dark bird whose life depends on creatures hiding under
stones
Beneath the torrents and foam
Through the icy grip of winter does he prevail
His bouncy step and piercing call mean life is here to remain
Amongst the boulders and leafless trees, the Dipper is the king
of his domain

The boulder-strewn river appeared lifeless; the chill of the winter morning still numbing the air as the mist rose from the swirling waters. The dank* mosses and lichen cladding the rocks provided the only colour to the greyness of the dawn. This was especially so as they were bedecked in a dusting of frost. The bare branches of the stunted sessile oaks pointed skywards like gnarled* witches' fingers into the blanket of grey. It seemed as though life had been sapped from the whole landscape, yet something was stirring amongst the foaming torrent: a high-pitched whistle accompanied by whirring wings and there he was, a resplendent Dipper, bobbing up and down with his white bib shining like a beacon—a true survivor of the winter.

He is a typical example of this species: somewhat chubby and squat, a perky short tail which is often held erect, his white throat and breast being demarcated by a bold chestnut brown border but it slowly darkens to almost black by the time it reaches his tail. His back, is a collection of dark browns with some of the feathers being edged with silver. The waterproof qualities of his plumage were shown by the few water droplets dripping off his back. His fairly long, thin black legs allow him to bounce on his long-toed feet. These long-taloned feet, despite being thin, are extremely powerful as they allow him to cling onto stones underwater as the powerful currents try their hardest to dislodge him during his feeding trips. He is forever restless, a bundle of nervous energy—a truly enigmatic* bird.

Dipper

However, he was not alone, as suddenly another bird appeared. It had a slightly different plumage: much darker, almost black, underparts which the first bird immediately noticed as the latter alighted on the neighbouring boulder.

"What are you doing on my stretch of river?" asked the first bird.

"I am dreadfully sorry to intrude," he said with a strange accent, "but I had no choice, my stream is completely frozen, I had to make a decision: stay and die or move to a warmer place. My name is Tyrian by the way," he answered, most politely.

"Hello Tyrian. I am known as Darcy. I have picked up a little accent, where are you from?"

"It is a place far away in the north, where in summer it is light 24 hours a day and the blackness of the winter nights is punctuated by brilliant displays of moving lights of every colour imaginable. I have heard humans call it aurora borealis* or the Northern Lights—a fine spectacle but it doesn't help me find food through those cold, bitter days. I believe that people call the country Norway, so I am a Viking, I guess!"

"I hope you are not here to pillage* the place!" said Darcy in the most sardonic* of voices.

"No, you can rest assured, I just need a place to stay over the winter," replied Tyrian.

"You have every right to find somewhere to survive, and fortunately, this river provides enough insect life for my family to get through these tough times. You are welcome to spend the winter here with us. How did you find your way here? I have never left the area, nor do I have any idea of what lies beyond these hills and steep tors*," admitted Darcy.

"Well, in Norway, my river flows in torrents as the snows melt in the spring, and further down the valley it meets the sea in craggy fjords.* These inlets are alive with fish, birds and seals. There are even howling wolves in the nearby evergreen forests, but all is not well."

"Why is that?" Darcy asked inquisitively.

"It has been a gradual process and stories from my forefathers say that the crystal-clear air slowly began to change. There was a smoky odour, almost undetectable, but with our heightened senses, they knew something was different: there were signs that things were changing. The tips of the conifer trees began to turn brown and slowly, but surely, this dieback increased until the trees sickened and eventually died. Not only that, the pure water tumbling down the mountain sides began to have an acidic tang*, the caddisflies began to disappear along with other tiny invertebrates*. In the worst places, my species could no longer survive. Many moved away and never returned; I really do not know what happened to them.

"I believe things are slowly getting better as there seems to be less air pollution; perhaps man is producing energy differently. If that is the case, then things should get better. We, are specialists, and it only takes a slight alteration to our environment to make us suffer. The most ironic thing is that the Dipper is the national bird of Norway, yet we are facing a lot of problems. Why are humans such foolish creatures?" Tyrian asked in a rather frustrated voice.

"I agree. They have made many idiotic blunders: I have heard that further down this river, the fish have all perished as a farmer acted irresponsibly by allowing some slurry to seep into the water which meant everything was wiped out," said Darcy.

"Slurry? What's that? It's a word I have never heard before."

"Sorry, I forgot you are not from around here. Slurry, hmm what's the best way to describe it? When farmers keep cows in a shed they have to clean up the mess they produce—often, they build tanks to store it in, but sometimes, these overflow and the brown, toxic liquid runs away and gets into the rivers and streams."

"You are talking bull! Yes?" replied Tyrian, helpfully.

"Yes. I thought you said your English was not that good! Well, where was I? Fortunately, this valley is owned by a recluse* who manages the woodlands, he ensures that everything remains as it should. I assume he decided to leave the hustle and bustle of the city behind thinking the best legacy he could provide would be a biosphere* which is self-sustaining and one teeming with life. He doesn't allow hunting, and that's why there is so much here. If only there were a few more people like him."

"You are absolutely right," Tyrian retorted.

Buzzard

Suddenly, a loud *mew* caused both Dippers to look up to see a Buzzard soaring above the valley; his finger-tipped wings helped him to maintain perfect control of the elements. His plaintive catcalls were answered by a female and the birds danced together. "Spring is coming—the first signs are the Buzzards pairing up and displaying."

"Where I live, the Raven is the mythical creature whose return heralds the spring; it means that the snow will soon be gone, and the plants will once again peek out amongst the scree* slopes."

Just then, a loud *honking* sound could be heard and, sure enough, the large formidable shape of a jet-black Raven appeared; he then began to tussle with the slightly smaller Buzzards, a superb aerial display of parrying* and swooping showed how manoeuvrable both species are. "The Raven is just showing his dominance; his partner is already sitting on eggs somewhere on the craggy heights. Why they choose to breed so early is beyond me. Perhaps, it is timed to the lambing season when there are plenty of opportunities to grab carrion or hunt effectively," said Darcy, who had probably answered his own question.

Raven

"Despite their very menacing looks, they do seem to have a sense of humour and a love of life as I have seen them frolicking in the snow and even sliding downhill on their backs with their legs in the air! I have actually seen them flying upside down just for the fun of it." Tyrian thought it was worth mentioning.

"I didn't know that," said Darcy, somewhat surprised.

"I have noticed that your seasons are so much earlier than where I come from. I cannot believe that even in the depths of winter, things are still growing, albeit slowly. I remember one winter at home, when the ice was so thick that I even had to resort to hunting under the ice, a very perilous endeavour and one I decided never to repeat. That's why I took the decision to come here. After all, the journey here was extremely difficult: flying for hours over a salty sea and then, when I was approaching land, there was a throng of menacing Gulls trying to force tired migrants into the sea. I saw a poor Blackbird being drowned just a few yards from the safety of the shore. I was utterly dismayed by what I saw but the Gulls were merciless; they seemed to be enjoying themselves. I believe many of their victims were not even pecked at once they met their demise*. What evil creatures they are!" Tyrian exclaimed.

"I quite agree. It is not easy here either, you know, foolish humans have altered our rivers too. They have allowed numerous non-native species to run amok. There is an evil 'American devil' here, called the mink. They have an insatiable* appetite, and during our breeding season, I have to be especially vigilant to ensure that I am not seen returning to my nest. So many broods have been obliterated by their nefarious* intentions. Why did so-called do-gooders think it necessary to 'liberate' these creatures from fur farms; they have unleashed a monster which is a threat to every bird and small mammal in the valley. Had they known the repercussions* of releasing these voracious* creatures into the wild, then maybe they would have acted differently. Ignorance is a classic failing of humans," Darcy said despondently.

Both birds shrugged their shoulders in unison.

"You are not alone in that opinion as everyone I speak to relates a similar story: nothing is allowed to stay the same, which is such a shame." Tyrian added.

"That's the way it is in the modern world. I have heard traditional stories, passed down from generation to generation, about a time before mechanisation and industrialisation when there were fewer humans around. In those days, man's influence on the planet was restricted to a few areas and everything seemed to work well. Without their machines, they couldn't tear up the earth so effectively and use the marginal lands for their farms. Oh, for those days to return!" Darcy sighed.

"I couldn't agree more!" replied Tyrian, nodding his head.

The surrounding woodland was silent, none of the birds were singing, except for a Robin whose melancholic winter song was proclaiming his territory and warning others to keep away.

"It's ironic that this is the most popular bird here and humans think they are cute. That red breast is just not an adornment; it's a warning. I have seen Robins battling to the death just to maintain their reign over a small hedgerow.

It seems excessive, but then again, I have been known to throw my weight around to ensure that any potential usurper* knows he's not wanted on my stretch of water during the breeding season."

"Absolutely! We need a certain amount of space to feed our families. Anyway, I think I'll stretch my wings a bit. I'm sure we'll have a chat before I fly back."

With that, Tyrian flew upstream until he disappeared around a bend.

Darcy looked up at the woodland above and saw a flock of Winter Thrushes: large grey-rumped Fieldfares cackling to each other as they made their forays into the berry-laden bushes nearby. Associated with them were the petite Redwings whose thin, *seeping* calls could be heard from a distance. Their russet sides and yellow eyebrows ensured they looked extremely dapper* as they sat atop the ancient oaks.

"How's life with you?" Darcy shouted out.

The most vociferous* of them answered. "We are just fine. Another mild winter and a good berry yield, what more could you wish for? At least there are a lot of them at the moment. Obviously, the Waxwings didn't bother to make the journey this year."

"Who?" questioned Darcy as he had never encountered this species before.

"The Waxwings; perhaps they never make it into this valley. They are the size of a Starling but are bright orangey pink with long crests and have a long carrying trill which is the wildest of sounds. Usually, they arrive in large flocks when the food sources at home fail, and they eat everything! In some languages Waxwings are called the plague bird!" replied the Redwing helpfully.

Waxwing

"Do they have the plague?" asked Darcy innocently.

"No! It's because they arrive en masse like a swarm of locusts. They are called Waxwings because they have tiny red feathers in their wings that look like drops of sealing wax. I have seen 50 birds in just one bush! The berries do not last long when they are around, I can tell you. Their attractive plumage does provide a lot of colour in the winter, but they do make our lives more difficult."

"Yes, I can imagine that would make life slightly more tiresome. There are not many of you this year, is there a problem?"

"No, many of my friends and relatives don't bother to migrate across the North Sea any more. As the winters are not so severe nowadays, they are prepared to take the risk and see the winter through on the mainland. It does save a perilous migration, perhaps I shall think of staying there in future.

"I have seen a few other birds here doing just the same. I met a Blackcap the other day, who told me she no longer flies to southern Spain or Northern Africa but feels that the British winter is not such a threat anymore and, with the kindness of some people, who put out fat balls and seed, ensures that there is always enough to eat despite the lack of insect life. She says more and more local birds are remaining here along with many migrant Blackcaps from Germany. She also told me that these German visitors are evolving: their beaks are getting thinner so that they can access these foodstuffs from the bird feeders much easier! It's remarkable how quickly birds can adapt to their surroundings and be successful. (There are many examples of birds evolving within a few generations.) All we need is a little time," the Redwing explained. With that he flew off to join his flock feeding nearby.

Slowly, as the days lengthened, the woods began to change: buds appeared on the lifeless twigs and the valley echoed to the resident birds proclaiming the changing of the seasons. The Song Thrush, pure of voice, whistled his song thrice repeating his stanzas*. A male Blackbird with his rich collection of warbling brought a depth of sound to the undergrowth.

The amelioration* of the climate means they have to start breeding earlier to ensure that their chicks have the best chance of survival. Birds are the final indication that huge changes are happening: the microscopic animals are altering their breeding patterns and the larger insects have had to adapt theirs, too. Throughout the food chain, things are not the same. The most obvious clue to the human eye is the behaviour of the larger creatures. Those interested in nature realise that there is a major shift occurring on an unprecedented scale.

Farther down the valley, amongst a copse* of large trees, there was a lot of activity; a constant hubbub of cawing as birds were trying to renovate their nests from the previous autumn. Although the trees were totally leafless and lifeless, these birds were really beginning their nest building in earnest. The Rooks were a sign to others that perhaps the worst of the winter weather had passed, but often, their travails* were in vain when heavy snowfall or howling gales destroyed the boughs and branches on which they had built their sturdy constructions. The Rooks, jet black with white bills, like this communal way of nesting; perhaps it adds a little more security, but these large birds don't really seem unduly threatened.

Unlike the black-billed Crow, this species is less of a threat to other smaller birds: they normally feed on the ground looking for all kinds of insects. The Crow and Magpie, however, actively seek out other birds' nests to steal their eggs or eat the young birds. Unfortunately, both these crows seem to have thrived in the more urban environments and obviously have had a negative impact on garden birds. Notwithstanding, the rookery showed that, despite the inclement weather, it was a centre of activity and for many, a true sign that spring was not far away.

Soon the spring equinox occurred, Tyrian bade his fond farewells to his new-found friends and then headed north-eastwards towards his fjords to the stretch of river which he called home. The resident Dippers were busy displaying and preparing for a hectic spring and summer when all their energy and attention would be needed to raise yet another family.

Waxwing

Spring Arrives

The frosty fingers at last relent, the winter's icy winds are spent
Finally, the greenery appears in a myriad* of subtle shades
Which soon would provide cool, sheltered, glades
Birds from afar begin to appear
To fill the air with their cheerful tones, so dear
Another season has begun,
A truly busy time for each and every one.

Wood Warbler

The days slowly began to lengthen, the catkins (named after cat tails) appeared on the Willows, giving some indication to all that the icy grip was relenting and milder conditions would soon prevail.

The volume of song increased as all the birds wanted to set up home and to attract a mate. In the conifers, the brick-red male and yellow-green female Crossbills were collecting bark strips from the silver birches to line their nests. These chunky finches' *chipping* calls echoed through the narrow valleys.

"Why do you breed so early?" asked a local Chaffinch.

"Well, we are so specialised—just look at my strange crossed beak; it is designed to open pine cones. We need the maximum amount of food available to feed our young and so our lives are dependent on when the trees produce their seeds. Hence we start breeding before other birds as we have to follow the natural rhythm of the pine trees otherwise our chicks won't have enough food to fledge," he replied.

Male Crossbill

"That makes sense," he remarked thoughtfully. "I really didn't know how dependent you are on just one particular food source and it is incredible that evolution has provided you with such a special beak to crack open the pine cones. I shall leave you to your work." The Chaffinch flew off towards the broadleaf woodland.

Goldfinch

Nearby was a beautifully-coloured Goldfinch with his black and red head with golden flashes in his wing that shone in the morning sun. He was busy constructing his lichen-clad nest in a conifer. His twittering could be heard through the surrounding woodland; it sounded like little bells. Despite his beauty, the nest would be a disaster by the time the youngsters left. Why they allow their nest to become caked with droppings is inexplicable; a possible explanation is that the noxious smell could keep predators away.

The various Tit species were busily chasing each other. The diminutive Blue Tit was calling loudly trying to attract a mate while the leafless landscape echoed to the Great Tit's teecha, teecha call. Both these species start nesting very early in the spring in this woodland, their lives had been made easier as the landowner had erected many nest boxes; as a result these birds were thriving in their new accommodation. Both species were picking up moss, feathers, cobwebs and discarded* wool from the sheep field nearby—using these materials to construct a snug cup inside the box.

Their young would be fledging in mid-May so there was a busy time ahead. Thousands of small, green caterpillars would be sacrificed to provide the nourishment for their broods. Sadly, a large proportion of their young leaving the nests would feature on many other birds' menus, and that is the reason why each pair would try to produce nearly a dozen young in a good season. These little birds do not live very long, therefore, they need to produce enough young to keep their numbers stable.

Blue Tit

Slowly, the woodland began to fill with the sounds from Africa as new species arrived from their massive migration. Darcy welcomed them all, as he did every year. The first was a Chiffchaff whose onomatopoeic* song echoed through the valley.

"Welcome back, old friend. How was your winter?" Darcy enquired enthusiastically.

"Not bad. I decided not to fly to Spain this year. I had the feeling that it wouldn't be necessary, so I flew down to the coast where the temperatures are kinder, and I found a treatment works which is always warmer than elsewhere. Naturally, there was always a constant supply of insects. Mind you, the smell was pretty nauseating but hey-ho! It saved me a thousand-mile round trip, and now, here I am, top fit and ready to find the prettiest girl, he boasted.

"I am sure she will arrive soon, but if she has been to Spain, she will be extremely tired when she arrives. I shall just have to bide my time and get back to my singing *chiff chaff, chiff chaff.*"

Up, upon the craggy tor, stood a stunning male Wheatear, his plumage truly resplendent in the spring sunshine, his black mask and white rump gleaming.

He pumped his tail and began to sing a melancholy song which drifted down to the torrents below. Darcy knew that the breeding season had begun.

"Welcome back Jude! How are you?" Darcy yelled out. Jude, on hearing his familiar voice, flew down to join him on the river bank.

"Fine. I'm glad to be back. The winter quarters in southern Spain are becoming inhospitable," Jude explained sadly.

"Why's that?" asked Darcy in an inquisitive voice.

"Well, that area of the country has not had much rain in the last few years; it's becoming more and more arid. It seems that desertification* is moving northwards so I am facing a great dilemma: do I stay in the north and face cold weather, or do I head south across the vast deserts to find an ideal spot for the winter?" Jude uttered worryingly.

"I see what you mean. I realise that my staying here, despite the risks, is better than journeying into the unknown."

"Not only that," Jude continued, "but the flight is fraught with difficulties. The humans on the other side of the Channel seem different, and everywhere there are invisible mist nets* from which no bird ever escapes alive. I once got caught a few miles from here, and all my nightmares came flooding back: I thought I was going to die. Surprisingly, I was gently taken out of the net and put in a white cotton bag; of course, my mind was racing and so was my pulse! I have seen thousands of birds disappear forever. A few minutes later, I was grabbed by a warm hand and I was lifted out. A metal ruler was placed on my outer wing, and then the human wrote some numbers in a special lined book. I was held upside down and put in a plastic funnel with a spring-like device attached. After a few seconds and more number writing, a metal ring was placed around my leg, with that I was gently released.

"See, I still have it! I don't know what it signifies, but I have met many birds who bear the same type of ring. I suppose people find it useful to track my journey should I be caught by some sympathetic person who is doing the same kind of study."

Jude then stuck out his leg to show his metal attachment which sparkled in the sunlight and, with that, he flitted away to begin his courtship song once again.

Suddenly, a triple whistling call pju, ju, ju could be heard above the gurgling waters of the river when a stiff-winged brown wader appeared from around the bend. He alighted near Darcy, called once again, bobbing and curtseying as he landed.

"You are back safe and well!" exclaimed Darcy, greeting the Common Sandpiper gleefully.

Common Sandpiper

"Greetings, young sir. Yes, I am back safe and well to face another summer amongst the torrents. It was a frightful journey as ever, but at least this year I was graced with fine weather, so I could make my northward journey fairly well. I am exhausted but once I rest and feed up, I shall be full of beans as usual. Am I the first?"

"Indeed, you are, but I am sure the others will arrive soon to keep you company. No doubt we'll meet up, and you can tell me all about your adventures."

The Sandpiper took off to find a safe place to roost, being alone for a while, Darcy ran into the waters to probe around for a tasty morsel to eat.

As the days lengthened, the sun's formerly feeble rays began to penetrate the gloomy depths of the forest, more colours began to appear. The yellow cowslips were superseded by the deep hues of the bluebells. Colour was also returning in the avian* world with the arrival of the Redstarts and the piebald* beauty of the Pied Flycatchers whose melodious voice could be heard drifting through the oak woods. Each new species heralded a new beginning and an indication that spring had truly arrived.

The beech trees, smooth of bark and clothed in brown leaves, suddenly began to shed their dry, brown foliage—remnants of the previous year. The brown buds began to split and then a sliver of green, the brown covering, thin as sugar paper, began to peel back and the emergent leaves unfurled: crinkled and weak at first, but slowly, as they became hydrated, grew larger and much prouder. With this metamorphosis*, their most brilliant green foliage brought a wonderful addition to the mid-May landscape. The ash and oak would soon follow to bring the final part of the magnificence of the spring.

Darcy was just about to dive into the raging torrent when he noticed an old friend flying up stream, his lemon underparts reflecting in the quieter areas of the water. His undulating flight and ridiculously long tail meant that the Grey Wagtail had returned to his breeding habitat. He settled down on a nearside rock, tail wagging incessantly, and gave a smile.

"Good to be back, Twitcher?" questioned Darcy.

"Of course, it is a new season with more challenges. Everything much the same here?"

"Yes, of course, the river is still flowing, the insects are emerging, and life is getting easier by the day. Did you have a good winter?" Darcy enquired.

Grey Wagtail

"Yes, I did the usual: I went down nearer to the coast and spent my time feeding on the flat roofs of the houses in the town. It's much warmer down there, you know, each house emits some heat and also, there are usually puddles in which to find some insects. I don't suppose many people actually know I am around. My cousins, the Pied Wagtails, are much more obvious, especially in the evenings when many fly into the city streets to roost in a particular tree under the lights. I counted over 100 there one evening, and many people just stop and stare as they cannot imagine why all these little black and white birds would choose to spend the night above a busy street. But then again, these people are just not aware how much warmer the city streets are compared to the countryside," explained Twitcher.

"I must admit it does get pretty cold up here but because the river is flowing so quickly, it just does not freeze over, and so my larder is always available. We had a visitor this year from Norway—he was forced to flee as his stream was covered in ice. We had a long chat about life in the far north, so I am grateful that I can spend the whole year here and just watch the world go by," reflected Darcy.

"I know what you mean, but it is easier for me to flee to slightly warmer conditions. Well, I suppose I should start collecting moss to build my nest. I think I will build it next to the little waterfall upstream; it looks a good spot. Where are you nesting this year?"

"I thought I would build my new home behind the larger waterfall. It will be out of sight and the noise of the rushing water means that no one can hear the screaming kids when they want feeding! I am sure that's why I have been so successful in the past. Why change the habit of a lifetime?"

"I totally agree. No doubt we will meet up during the season. Better get started!"

"I should be doing the same. See you in a while."

A few weeks later, a pju pju pju was quickly followed by a snake-like hissing, descending rattle coming from the beech trees; it heralded the return of the Wood Warbler to its territory. His penetrating song echoed through the awakening forest; his pure white belly and yellow bib made him unmistakable amongst the emerging green leaves. Not only was his rattling call diagnostic but his parachuting display flight between the trees made sure that every inhabitant in the woods knew he was back on the block. All the other creatures welcomed him back and asked about his winter adventures.

"How are you, Elkwood?" asked a nosey Thrush who was perched nearby.

"Fine, another dreadful journey but it's wonderful to see the verdant* colours of this woodland. My journey seems to be getting worse each time I make it; the barren landscapes seem to be getting larger, and the humans are becoming more common in areas where once they were rare. The bushes and cover are being stripped by their wild stock, especially their goats, who are wiping out many small shrubs. Without adequate cover, we are all at risk as there are predators everywhere awaiting any chance to catch a meal. Not only are there hunters on the ground, but there are also numerous hunters on the wing. I have had to adapt my roosting habits to make sure I have some form of protection. Normally, I return fit and healthy despite the huge journey but after an anxiety-filled winter with a lack of proper sleep,

I feel exhausted and now I have to put all my energy into finding a mate," answered Elkwood wearily.

"Wow! That is dreadful. I am lucky, I can eke out a living here during the short days of winter; it seems better to struggle here than suffer your travails*."

"Don't worry, it's great to be back amongst these wonderful woods and experience the long days of summer. I am quite optimistic on it being another successful season."

As May turns to June, the frenetic* pace of life changes: the woodlands become much quieter; the southern songsters do not spend their energy proclaiming their presence as they have hungry mouths to feed. The woodlands become filled with chips and *cheeps* of begging youngsters but otherwise, the tuneful melodies have almost disappeared. The warmth of the season has brought a quieter period within the forested glens. It is a time for consolidation and educating the newly-emerged fledglings to find their own food and learn the survival skills they will need in life—such an important task.

Family Life

Darcy started calling and displaying and he was soon joined by an attractive female and, as he went through his bobbing courting ritual, she showed that she was interested in him.

"Would you like to raise a family together? I have the perfect spot to set up home," he proclaimed proudly.

"Yes, that sounds fine. Show me where it is," Charlize answered enthusiastically.

"Follow me."

They took off together and he showed her a few places where he had already started a few nests but eventually, she decided that the perfect place would be under the waterfall, exactly the spot which Darcy had always wanted. Charlize obviously knew it would be the safest haven as the rushing torrents would shield her from the rest of the world.

"I shall have to put a few finishing touches and then I think it will be perfect!"

"Of course, my dear, whatever you say," he replied.

Over the next few days, the final accessories were added to the nest and then she laid four pure-white eggs in the moss-filled bowl. Then began the long period of incubating, each taking it in turn to ensure that the eggs remained warm, and finally, after about three weeks, the eggs began to crack and four pink, blind, naked chicks sat there, almost reptile-like but already hungry. Immediately after hatching, Darcy took the egg shells away and disposed of them some way from the nest; he really did not want to leave any signs that there was a nest nearby.

A Dipper, hard at work

He had to do most of the hunting at the beginning as his partner had to stay with the helpless chicks to keep them warm. The position of the breeding site meant there was a constant spray of water droplets falling into the nest, and it would have been foolhardy to leave her naked brood alone to freeze.

Darcy spent every minute of the daytime flying underwater and using his long toes and nails to cling onto rocks as the powerful river would try to wash him away if he wasn't careful. He used his beak to move pebbles, and his keen eyesight would pick up any aquatic insect life hiding underneath. His favourite quarry* was the caddisfly which was well camouflaged as it had built itself a coat of armour from tiny stones to protect its soft body. As these tiny stones had been collected from the river bed, they blended in perfectly with the bottom of the river. Despite this, the Dipper's perseverance and knowledge ensured he had the skills to outwit these insects. Once he had found one, he would scamper out of the raging waters, stand on a stone and break through the stony armour to reveal the naked insect. After he had made sure that nobody was looking, he would fly back to the nest, hop through the waterfall and present his dinner to his partner who would then feed the chicks with his offering. This routine was performed hundreds of times a day.

Slowly but surely, the naked pink bodies became covered in dark primitive feathers, more like the spines of a hedgehog when they first appeared but gradually, they unfurled to become fluffy. Now the chicks could be left alone as they were now able to retain their body heat. As they grew, so did their demand to be fed, therefore, both parents had a busy time searching the river bed for food. There was not a moment to relax as there was always a potential threat that the nest could be discovered by a fox, polecat or mink. The birds always had to be vigilant and aware that somewhere, there could be a pair of eyes watching their antics. Fortunately, owing to the site of the nest under the cascading waters, the youngsters' begging cries were hardly audible—both parents knew that their growing offspring were always hungry, and they were well aware that they had a busy schedule to keep.

Meanwhile, just down the river, the same story was being played out by Darcy's friend, Twitcher. Both birds were hunting flying insects emerging from the quieter areas of the river. They too were exhausted but they were also successful in raising their chicks. A very pleasing season indeed.

Finally, after nearly a month of incessant activity, Darcy's youngsters had grown all their waterproof feathers, they were ready to face the world. On a sunny late spring day, the birds ventured out of the nest to see the glistening river which would be their home from now on. Darcy and Charlize fed the birds outside the nest for some time and, once the fledglings had learnt how to hunt for themselves, the parents could relax for the first time in months.

"Wow! That was a busy time, wasn't it!" Darcy muttered to Charlize in an exhausted voice.

"You can say that again!" she uttered wearily.

"At least they are now independent and can find their own way in life. We have been lucky; they all survived, it is up to them now to get through the demanding autumn and winter, if they manage that, then they will become the kings and queens of this river once we are no longer here," she said somewhat smugly.

"Well done. We have done a great job, and I am proud of what we have achieved. I guess it is now time to go our own ways."

She nodded wistfully*. They embraced each other before returning to their old lives.

Dipper

The Wheatear and the Peregrine

Talons sharp, and watchful eye, the fastest creature ever to fly
Meets a journey man from the Deep South and together
They chat about things so dear
That even the Wheatear loses his fear
Two different worlds collide but
Both have problems they need to tell
And, for a moment, at least, they get on well.

Peregrine Falcon

Back on the craggy slopes, high above the foaming river, Jude was singing and showing off his white rump when he peered over the edge of the precipice and was somewhat surprised to see a female Peregrine Falcon sitting almost motionless on her eggs in a deep crevice on the vertical cliff.

"Oh!" he exclaimed. The female Falcon twisted her neck and looked at him with her jet-black eyes. The yellow rims to her eye sockets contrasted vividly against her black moustachial* stripes. Her long, hooked bill glistened in the sun.

"So, you are the one making all the noise here," she said in an unthreatening voice.

"Sorry if I disturbed you," he answered meekly. "I am Jude, the Wheatear and what do they call you?"

"I am known as Terra."

"You are new here, aren't you?"

"Yes, I am. My ancestors used to breed on this very cliff face I was told, but it has taken generations for us to return."

"Why, what happened to them?"

"Well, in the 1950s, man thought he had discovered the panacea* for the insect pest problem by developing some pesticides (DDT and dieldrin). It seemed to have the desired effect on the insects, but it took some time for the ramifications* of this action to become apparent. This poison was taken up by the surviving bugs which were, subsequently, eaten by hunting animals and birds—my species included," explained Terra.

"Did your ancestors die from the poison?"

"Well, some did, but as this poison moved up through the food chain, it became more concentrated and, as we are one of the top predators, we were the hardest hit. The long-term consequences were catastrophic for all the birds of prey and my species was reduced by around 90%, leading to local extinctions throughout our range." Terra related this story with a lump in her throat.

Jude moved closer, fascinated by this story. "What did it do? Why were you almost pushed to extinction?"

"Well, it affected the females, and the eggs we laid were paper-thin, and, as my ancestors sat down to incubate, the eggs just collapsed, killing the embryos inside. It did not take long for the population to crash as no new birds were being born to make up for our natural mortality rate," said the Falcon, with a tear in her eyes.

"Wow!" exclaimed Jude who was mortified by what he had just heard.

"We have enough problems as it is; we are the fastest creature on the planet, flying at 370 km per hour in a dive;

47

that has its own inherent risks as one slight flex of the wrong wing muscle could prove fatal. I have had many close calls chasing Pigeons, they are clever fliers, and I have nearly hit a branch or cliff face but luckily, I managed to gain control and avoid a collision," Terra explained.

"But you have returned to your old haunts. How is that possible?" asked Jude, who was incredibly inquisitive.

"Oh yes, well, fortunately, some people in this country are very interested in ornithology*, and they undertook a survey to count our numbers; they were shocked by our population crash. Scientists undertook experiments on our broken eggs, and they found huge concentrations of these toxic chemicals. It sent alarm bells ringing, especially as similar results had been found around the world. These chemicals were banned in the northern hemispheres and slowly, the problem dissipated* as the poisons washed away. It has taken over 50 years to recover and that, in tandem with a more educated population and reduced persecution, is why we have been able to return to our former haunts*. I believe there are about 1,500 pairs in the country today. We have even moved into their cities and, with the help of special nest boxes provided by the more enlightened people who realised we needed a little help, they now have a natural solution to their Pigeon problems! I must admit, I do enjoy a fresh Pigeon!"

Jude swallowed hard. Terra smiled and reassured him that he was not at risk as he wouldn't even be a snack! She also said she enjoyed his singing as there was not a lot of song high up on the moors.

Merlin

"You should have no fears from my husband and me, but you have to be very afraid of my mini cousin, the Merlin, as he is built to hunt small birds like you and your Pipit friends. We all have to live somehow, and no one is safe. Man has the capacity to affect the whole environment, as my story proves, but you should watch out, my little friend, as others have hungry chicks on the way, so always keep an eye out and maintain your vigilance 24 hours a day. It really is a tough world."

"Thank you for your warning, I shall certainly heed your advice. I saw a much smaller bird very similar to you yesterday sitting on this cliff. Is that your baby?" asked Jude.

Terra cackled with laughter. "Baby! No, that's my husband! I am sitting here on eggs, as the chicks haven't hatched yet."

"Why is he so much smaller?"

"Well, evolution is ingenious. He may be smaller but is more adept* than I am at catching faster, more agile birds whereas I am heavier and can take much bigger, slower prey, so together we make a great team! Also, he is a little afraid of me, and so he always gives up his food whenever I ask for it!"

"That's clever—who would have thought it!" said Jude, who was extremely surprised. "Do you have a new husband every year?"

"No, we usually stay together for most of our lives. If he is an excellent provider, why should I look for another? In a good year, we can produce up to four chicks," replied Terra.

"We often produce more than that, so why are you so proud of your mothering skills?"

"I don't know whether you are aware but many miles away, high in the mountains, is a pair of Golden Eagles and they really do live a long time, but they do not produce many chicks at all. They normally don't breed until they are six or seven years old; you'd be long dead by then! But because they find it difficult to find enough food, they only lay two eggs. The second egg hatches a week later so there is a big size difference between the youngsters. It is common that the smaller chick is eaten by his brother or sister! It's one way to provide a meal, I suppose, but it is usually enough to ensure that at least one bird is produced each year. Only in good years are two birds fledged, and so I am thrilled when I can produce four youngsters."

"Well, that really puts family life into perspective!" remarked Jude. "By the way, how long do your live?"

"Well, some of us live for about 30 years, so that is a lot of Pigeon pie! And you, are you married for life?"

"Alas, we have a fairly short life, and if we are extremely fortunate, we may live for ten years, but every year, I serenade this moorland and whoever returns, I shall start a family with her. Many birds do not survive the journey, so there is little point waiting in vain for my 'wife' to return.

"By the way, do all predatory birds differ in size?" asked Jude.

"No, only the Falcon species which hunt birds, so that's the aerial hunters including the Sparrowhawk and Goshawk. Birds which hunt mammals or insects do not need to be different sizes as they are specialised in hunting certain animals.

The Kestrel, despite being a Falcon, preys on mice, and therefore both sexes are the same size. Did you know that they are able to see in a different light spectrum which means they can see the urine marks of a mouse from a great height, and as these trails shine brightly for the Kestrel, he knows exactly where the mice have been and what paths they follow in the long grass? They are successful hunters because they have this specialised skill and the ability to hover in one spot, which is unusual in many predators.

Kestrel

"The moral to this story is, always wash your hands when you have been to the toilet! Don't worry; I won't tell the mice as I don't want my Kestrel friends to go hungry!"

"But you are a successful hunter—how do you do it?"

"Well, my eyes are superior to yours; I can see much better than you. They magnify the image, so I can see much farther than the average bird. I hunt using skill and speed. My nostrils are specially adapted so when I am diving on my prey at huge speeds, my lungs do not break, my heart is also altered to this high-speed life, so I do manage quite well."

"Wow! There is so much I didn't know. Do you stay here the whole year because, as you might know, I fly south in the autumn?"

"It depends, if there is enough food, I stay in the local vicinity, but I usually head to slightly warmer places down on the coast where there are vast flocks of ducks and waders, they keep me well-fed."

"What about your children?"

"Well, they usually spend some time with me as they have so much to learn. Hunting is not easy, and sometimes we hunt together so that they can learn the ropes. Once they feel confident enough to catch their own food, we go our own way. They spend a year or so moving around, honing* their skills and discovering the best place to start their own families. That's why either my husband or I return early in the year to make sure that no one is trying to take over 'our' cliff. Sometimes, there are a few words spoken to ensure they know their place, and then they go off to find another site. We need a certain amount of space to ensure we have enough to eat throughout the summer."

"That makes sense, I suppose," replied Jude after some consideration.

"Well, that's how it works in my world, my little friend," Terra said.

Suddenly, there was a high-pitched scream and high above, the male Falcon was circling, an item of prey in his talons. "Oh great, dinner has arrived! I was wondering what had happened to my little man!"

"Well. I'll leave you in peace to enjoy your meal. Thank you for the chat, it was most enlightening. Speak to you soon."

"It was a pleasure, but perhaps it would be better to come back when my husband is not around, as he may not be able to control his hunting urges. As I said, he does like hunting smaller birds!"

"I am very grateful for the warning!" and with that, Jude flitted away out of sight from Mr Peregrine.

Female Wheatear

The Pigeon and the Cuckoo

Little birds beware
There is a nefarious* creature in the air
Don't stray, stay where you are, don't fly away
For she, in your little nest, her egg will lay
Once this has been done, your life will never be the same
As you struggle to feed a stranger, in this awful game
Come the autumn it will fly away
The following year, it may return, and 'cuckoo' is all it will say

Tatum, the grey Wood Pigeon, was sitting on her untidy nest, busy keeping her brood warm, when a female Cuckoo suddenly perched on a nearby branch.

"Good morning to you," said Trix, the Cuckoo. "Are you well?"

Cuckoo

"I am fine, just trying to get the kids to sleep. They have been up since dawn, and it's time for them to have a little nap. How is your brood?" Tatum asked.

"No idea. I have never seen them."

"What! Never seen them! What an irresponsible mother you are! How can you be so heartless, how do they survive being all alone?"

"Well, you are obviously not familiar with my lifestyle! We do not do this parental responsibility act. I'd rather leave it to others to bring up my children; I am far too busy enjoying life," replied Trix nonchalantly.

"That's a rather selfish attitude to have, isn't it? What do you do with your kids and who do you leave them with?" asked Tatum.

"It depends on who is around. It could be a Dunnock, Reed Warbler or any other unsuspecting species."

"Don't they have problems with the other chicks?" Tatum was obviously worried about this arrangement.

"Of course not! There aren't any! We make sure we are alone in the nest so that our 'parents' will devote their time solely to us," Trix bragged.

"Well, how do you do that?"

"When we hatch, our first instinct is to eject any eggs or young from the nest, and we are really good at it, as you can see. When I was a few hours old, I remember using all my strength to push everything out of the nest. As a result, I did get well fed by my adopted parents."

"Why doesn't the bird realise that there is a strange egg in its nest?"

"It's all very clever, you see, I know which birds breed near here, and so I lay eggs which look almost exactly the same as my host's although they are slightly larger. I can change the colour to match the other eggs. It shows that birds are not very observant and they are only interested in raising young," she replied confidently shuffling her feathers as she spoke.

"You have never seen any of your children then?"

"No, not even one" was the abrupt reply. "I never met my parents so why should I care?"

"That is unbelievable. What a strange arrangement. What happens to you when you disappear in late summer, where do you go?"

"I have a long journey to central Africa. It is an arduous trip, but it is what I have to do to survive," she admitted.

"Do you at least help the youngsters to find their way back home to Africa?" Tatum asked expectantly.

"No, the adults leave much earlier than they do, so they have to find their own way."

"That must make their task even more frightening. How did you make your first journey alone?"

"I don't know, it's just a feeling. My instinct told me it was time to go: the days were shortening, and there was an ever-increasing chill to the air. Food was becoming scarcer and it was obvious I had to go. I spent weeks looking at the stars noticing how they moved. Perhaps I have an internal compass and clock. The sun plays an important part too, as I seem to know in which direction to fly. One day, I instinctively knew I had to head south and just keep flying until it felt right, and that's exactly what I did. I ended up in a bushy area in central Africa. It is amazing that when you put your mind to it, you can achieve anything."

"Do you come back to the same place?" asked Tatum, who was appalled by her mothering skills but, at the same time, intrigued by the story of her journey.

"Yes, I was born in this valley; my parents were a pair of Reed Warblers nesting in the reed-bed not far away."

"But how did you know where this valley was?"

"Well, in the few weeks after I left the nest, I spent my time flying around the local area remembering all the landmarks: the cliffs over there, the river, the estuary ten miles away and the coastline on both sides of it. I remembered the unique smells and the position of the stars. I also made a note of everything I saw on my long trip as I knew I would have to travel the same way back; every piece of information is vital. Somehow, I used all this data and found my way back here. The second time was much easier, as things were more familiar, and I knew how much food I would need to sustain me through this arduous journey."

"That is an amazing story," Tatum admitted. "I often move away in large flocks in the autumn when the weather closes in, so we do not have to concentrate too much. It is also easier to travel in a group as we all help each other. Our biggest threat is the Falcons who often attack our flocks but compared to your story, I feel somewhat humbled. I do not approve of your parenting skills, but your journey does fill me with admiration; you really are a special bird."

"Thank you for your compliment, but I have to be off as I need to lay another egg before the end of the day." With that, Trix flew off strongly, heading towards the reed bed looking for a suitable host for her egg.

The birds who were familiar with the Cuckoo raised the alarm by shrieking their warning cries. Suddenly, many birds arose to mob the female, and so she carried on flying into the distance—perhaps her egg was not laid that day.

Cuckoo

High Fliers

A scythe-shaped form, black as ink, appears from afar
A banshee* call, a little roll on those absurdly long wings
Winter has gone and now is spring
A time for others to sing
Yet the Swift just keeps on flying to feed,
Everything done at break-neck speed
The true sign that the harbinger of summer is here, indeed

Swift

The final sign of the spring was when the scythe-shaped wings of the Swift could be seen over the valley. Their screams were the true sound of summer. A Swallow, flying high above the valley, was the first to greet the birds.

"Hello, good to see you back, Turpin," she said in a relieved voice.

"Greetings, Harper. It's good to be back, although we are only here for three months. I do not know where my real home is, as I spend more time abroad than I do here, but at least these long days allow us to raise our chicks," Turpin answered.

"Have you built your nest yet?" Harper enquired.

"No, not really. I have returned to the house where I raised my family last year; the old nest is still there unscathed*. It's a bit difficult for us to gather nesting material as I cannot perch in a tree or land on the ground."

"I didn't know that. Why can't you perch?"

"Well, I do not have any legs to speak of. I cannot walk at all, and if I fall to the ground, I am doomed. My wings are so long, and my legs are so short that I cannot leap into the air, I will never get airborne again. Not a very dignified way to go, is it?" Turpin said with a frown.

"No, I suppose not. So where do you roost?"

"We don't roost! We fly up thousands of feet and then just circle round and round to snatch some sleep. When we get a bit low, we fly up again and repeat it. We really are busy creatures; I fly nearly 900 km daily when I am searching for food, especially when the weather is bad, I will seek out the best place to feed and that could be a long way away. I sometimes fly over to Europe for the day if the weather here is dreadful, as the kids need to be fed, you know. We are not here very long, usually arriving in late April and leaving at the end of July, so we don't have enough time to raise two families in a season. But travelling so far everyday means I am really familiar with the local area which ensures I can find 'home' after being away for most of the year. When I left my nest the first time, I did not sit down for four years. We don't start breeding until we are four and our lifespan is about ten years although I've heard that the oldest ringed bird was over 21! We are made to fly and that is what we do! I will probably fly nearly two million miles in my lifetime."

"That is remarkable! I thought I flew a long way but it's nothing compared to you," conceded Harper.

"Talking about nests, my neighbours, some House Martins, are really clever; their mud constructions are a work of art.

House Martin

"I often see them waddling around, collecting mud and then flying to the wall, near my entrance hole under the roof, where they use their incredible skills to produce a beautiful piece of pottery. I do not know if they add anything to the mud, but it seems to be incredibly strong, especially in late summer when their young are really quite big. These nests seem to last for years so they must be extraordinary." Turpin conceded.

"Yes, they really do a fantastic job. My nest is a bit of a mess to be honest; we usually construct our nests inside a building, preferably on a beam, we collect a few feathers, cobwebs, bits and bobs and add them to the mixture. It meets our needs and sometimes, if it is a good season, we raise two families but it all depends on the spring weather. I remember a dreadful late May a few years ago; it was bitterly cold and wet; as there were no insects on the wing, my husband and I could not find enough to eat. My poor babies could not survive; it was heart breaking, but we started again and, as the weather improved, we were successful with our second brood. I hear there was a huge mortality rate during that early spring and most babies died. There seems to have been a shift in the weather patterns recently: summer storms are more common, torrential rains and gales seem more frequent—a sign that things are changing?

"My cousins, the Sand Martin, arrive even earlier than I do, so they really do take a risk with the fickle* March weather. They are the first aerial insect-feeders to get here, spending a lot of their time hunting their prey over stretches of water—how they survive the frosty weather is beyond me. Have you visited one their colonies?" Harper enquired.

"No, I cannot say that I have, why?" answered Turpin.

"Well, it really is something. They nest in sandy cliff faces.

Sand Martin

"Most years they excavate a new hole, spending hours shifting sand to make a burrow, hence the name Sand Martin. In a large colony, the cliff face looks like a sponge! I suppose they enjoy each other's company, perhaps it is a safer way to nest? Of course, their predators know exactly where to find them! Their greatest threat comes from the Hobby, which is a really agile flier, who follows them from Africa.

"Normally, Hobbies are quite happy catching dragonflies, which they eat on the wing, but I am sure there is more nourishment in a Sand Martin. We all have our problems, I suppose," Harper said in a resigned voice.

"Anyway, back to your story, I find it incredible that you only sit down when you are incubating eggs; you really are the ultimate flying machine. Just another question—it's a little embarrassing, but how do you do 'it'?" she blushed after asking that question.

"The same as you, but we do 'it' on the wing like everything else we do! I told you, we really are the masters of the skies. Our screaming may be one of the only reasons that people look up and notice us. We are even called the devil bird because of that demonic sound, but for others, it is the epitome of summer," Turpin answered full of pride.

"Well, I am finding it difficult keeping up with you, and I am getting dreadfully tired. I'll let you get back to your feeding, I wish you a good season. Let's hope the weather is favourable so we can all be contented parents in a few weeks' time."

The Swift thanked her, said his goodbyes, and then sped off at breakneck speed towards the town, screaming like a banshee as he went. Harper caught a few flies, then landed on a fence to catch her breath and take the opportunity to relax awhile. She could appreciate the joys of sitting and relaxing in the sunshine whereas the poor Swift could never experience that simple pleasure. She burst into her babbling song just to show how happy she was.

Swallow

Autumn Approaches

A chill in the air, a sign of change
Summer songsters aware they are now beyond their range
Time to leave before the frost begins to bite
This is the time for flight
To warmer sites far to the south
While those who remain will live from hand to mouth
The spangled* leaves and autumn tints
Are more than just hints
That the trees are about to hibernate
Leave now before it's too late
And forsake* this place with its ghostly mists
The shortening days mean there is no time to desist

Slowly, the days begin to shorten with a new crispness in the air; the summer songsters who had raised their offspring are growing restless; obviously something is stirring within their bodies; some of their organs shrink as they are no longer needed. Most moult their old flight feathers following the breeding season so that they will have a perfect new set when it comes to migrating or facing the winter. They spend the whole day feeding up and laying down fat ready for their departure. They will need every milligram to propel them to their destination thousands of miles away. Some would take a sedate, short-jump form of migration, stopping off at various sites on the way, feeding up once again and then continuing on their journey. Others, such as the Cuckoo, would fly massive distances in a few days before resting up a little while and then making another long non-stop flight over the Sahara before reaching central Africa.

Even fairly similar species, such as the Reed and Sedge Warbler, use different strategies in their migration method.

The former takes a non-stop flight from their breeding site to northern Spain, where they take their first break. The latter takes numerous stops on their way south, migrating a few miles every day. The traditional stopping off points must be protected as they are vital feeding and roosting sites for these tiny birds. Without them, these birds would not survive the huge journey.

As each day passes, another species goes missing, the woodlands become much quieter. In early autumn, this is not so obvious as other birds arrive from further north. They may stay a few days but soon even they have passed through. The colourful spring plumages of most birds have been discarded for a more subtle colour scheme—perhaps a strategy to make them less obvious during the winter, meaning that they are not such a colourful target for other predators.

The skies above the valley are full of twittering Swallows and Martins, but there is now a purpose in their flight; no longer are they fluttering around lazily feeding on flying insects. They all pass in large flocks heading southwards, and within a couple of weeks, the sky is empty and so it will stay for another six months.

The autumn tints on the broadleaf woodlands echo this feeling: a sign that life is slowing down, the trees are entering a dormant phase. The misty mornings also reflect this season of melancholy and despite its beauty, the autumn is a prelude for the forthcoming winter.

Ring Ouzel

The arrival of the Autumn Thrushes in October is the true sign that the colder days are not far away. The *chak chak* of a visiting Ring Ouzel, who had moved down off the high moorlands, shows that the season's clock is ticking on remorselessly*: he will stay a few days to feed up on the autumn berries before moving south to spend his winter, probably in the Atlas Mountains of Morocco.

The Grey Wagtails would soon be moving to lower altitudes, leaving just the Dippers to hunt through the dark, cold days of winter. A quietness descends upon the valley, the cacophony* of sound which accompanied the spring, a distant memory. The Robin begins his new winter song, quieter, more sombre in a minor key, perhaps reflecting the mood of the waning* year.

The undergrowth dies back, the verdant ferns now brown and decaying; discarded leaves dance in the air as the autumn winds race through the trees. The animals, preparing for their hibernation, seek out anything edible to store away in their caches*. A Jay is busying himself by collecting acorns and burying them just to make sure he has a store during the often-brutal days of the forthcoming season. Preparation is the key to survival.

Jay

The bare branches once again look like twisted fingers. The year has turned full circle.

Cliff Hangers

Twenty storeys high with breakers at your feet
Is a place thronged by thousands who in the summer months meet
To raise families on the perilous cliffs
Where one wrong movement could lead to doom
Because here there just isn't room
Cling on for life and that's what they do
Hoping the fish stocks will last to see them through
And once the cold winds blow, these stacks and the sea below
Are deserted once more to face the storms alone
Waiting until spring brings all the sea birds home

Puffin

Down on the coast, on the sheer granite cliffs, were row upon row of Razorbills and Guillemots all vying* for a few inches on which to lay their peculiar shaped eggs. Above them, on broader ledges, the Kittiwakes had built their guano*-stained nests, their evocative* calls reverberating all through the colony. There was a constant threat to all, as marauding* Great black-backed Gulls, Ravens and Herring Gulls were looking out for any unattended eggs which would be devoured before the neighbouring birds could react.

Guillemots

Also, amongst the throngs were Fulmars, the northern hemisphere's mini albatross, who sat passively on their nests, looking down on the busy coming and goings. Their stiff-winged, mechanical flapping showed that they were very different to any Gull. Their fairly heavy bodies and thick necks made them look like a flying cigar. Their peculiar tube-nosed beaks showed they were true oceanic birds.

On the lower slopes were the emerald green Shags with their piercing yellow eyes and distinctive shaggy crests, their nests a collection of flotsam and jetsam* bedecked with seaweed. Soon, their pterodactyl-like young would emerge from the eggs and the parents would be hard pressed to find enough fish to maintain their ever-growing chicks—an extremely difficult, if not impossible, task which is reflected by their 50% population decline over the last 25 years.

The sounds of all the squabbling birds of different species was deafening, but the overall sound was superseded by the constant crashing of the large Atlantic waves against the ancient strata*. The resultant spray shone like mini-prisms in the sun: millions of tiny rainbows adding to the beauty and dynamism of this breath-taking landscape.

At the top of the cliffs, amongst the grassy knolls, were the adorable Puffins, clown-like with their multi-coloured triangular beaks and bright orange feet. Unlike their relatives, the Guillemots and Razorbills, Puffins actually stand on their legs and walk well on the grassy slopes. His relatives use their legs as a cushion when they sit down but they shuffle around on their thighs in a rather ungainly manner. The Puffins' eggs were safely underground in abandoned rabbit burrows but, every now and then, one of the adults would come up to get some fresh air and fly out to sea to go fishing. However, the return trip was always an ordeal as the Gulls were waiting for them, and if they harassed the unfortunate bird long enough, he, or she, would drop the sand eels to provide them with an easy meal.

Often, the Puffins would stand around chatting to each other. "Are you well today, Asher?" asked one of his neighbours.

"Not bad, I suppose, but it is getting harder to find enough sand eels," he answered with a frown.

"I know. It seems that the fishermen are taking away our livelihood. The sea seems to be getting warmer, the currents are changing, meaning the fish are moving away from the shore. I now have to travel much greater distances than I did a few years ago. It's definitely getting more difficult to raise a family nowadays. Our numbers are crashing and that may be the reason why. Perhaps it would be better to move northwards where the fishing might be a little easier. The rat population seems to be increasing, we do not have a chance if they raid our nests. I have heard of places where humans have eradicated this menace, and the birds are now doing much better."

"Yes, I have heard of some of the positive steps they are taking on some small islands; if only they could do something here to give us some relief. Maybe there are better places to set up home, if the fish numbers continue to dwindle here, I may have to move as well." Asher admitted.

"Yes, something has to be done. Anyway, it's no use standing around chatting; I have to get something for everyone to eat." With that, his whirring wings took him over the edge of the cliff down towards the glistening sea below.

Offshore, there was a blizzard of white birds with distinctive back wing-tips and yellow heads, their large wing spans looking small from such a distance. Their lithe, streamlined bodies were perfect for their method of hunting. Suddenly, the flock came across a mackerel shoal and, almost at once, they folded their wings entering the water like arrows, without a splash—a perfect ten in any diving competition! A few seconds later, the birds bobbed up to the surface with fish in their beaks. They then became airborne, and the Gannets made their way homeward to their breeding colony some miles away. A spectacular exhibition of fishing at its best.

A Fulmar yawned and looked with her jet-black eyes at a neighbouring Kittiwake.

"Good day, Pearl. How is life with you today?"

"Mustn't complain, Chiselton. At least the sun is shining and it's not blowing a gale! Why do you look so very different to me? I must say I have never seen such a strange looking beak before. Why do you have those peculiar tubes?" Pearl wanted to know.

"Huh! If I didn't know you so well I would take offence. I shall enlighten you on the benefits of having such a specialist bill. The tubes, called naricorns, allow me to get rid of salt from my body, I have a special salt gland just behind them and so I can desalinate my body and even drink sea water without any ill effect like all true pelagic* birds. They also allow me to smell my prey on those huge oceans; I often eat floating carrion and having a good sense of smell makes that task much easier. I have met albatrosses and petrels on my journeys, and they all have similar beaks so I am not alone with this feature."

"Oh, I do apologise. I didn't intend to upset you."

"Don't worry, my skin is as thick as my beak! It is obviously a successful feature as we are very long-lived birds and probably travel thousands of miles per year, but that is nothing compared to the albatrosses. They are struggling like many others on these cliffs, you know."

"Really, what's their problem?" asked Pearl.

"Where do I start? As you know, they eat fish and they often follow trawlers looking for morsels. Unfortunately, these fishermen use fish as bait to catch tuna. They then put them on hooks attached to long lines but, as the baited hooks are released from the ships, the albatrosses dive down trying to get a free meal. Tragically, they get impaled on the hooks and drown. What a dreadful way to perish. It has been mentioned that steps have been taken to alleviate the problem: the back of the ships now have a long cover, so the baited lines sink too far below the surface for the albatrosses to reach, meaning they cannot be dragged underwater to their

Guillemots and Kittiwake

deaths. There are still problems with using fishing nets in the Southern Hemisphere as many birds meet their demise after getting caught in the mesh; what a deplorable way to die! In the larger albatross species their young stay a year in the nest, and are at risk from rats and many never reach the flying stage. Where man has taken steps to eradicate predators, their breeding success has improved."

"That's good to know, are there any other problems?"

"Actually, there are many! Pollution in the oceans is also another threat—especially plastics—which the birds often mistake for food. Many have been found with their stomachs full of synthetic items, which of course, destroy their digestive systems. There are uninhabited islands in the middle of the oceans covered in dangerous flotsam, metres deep; it's all extremely grim."

"Wow! I just didn't realise that there were problems so far out to sea! How do you find your way back to this cliff every year?"

"All seabirds have an incredible ability to navigate the featureless oceans; I suppose it's just something you are born with. I heard about a Manx Shearwater that was collected in Wales, taken to America where it was released and, believe it or not, he was back in his breeding burrow a few days later! Now, that's what I call wonderful navigation."

"That is truly amazing! You mentioned that you were long-lived; how long is long-lived?" Pearl wanted to know.

"Well, I know some of us live for about 70 years. One ringed bird even exceeded that—so that is a long time! But don't forget, we take a few years before we are old enough to breed, during this time we explore the oceans and the coastlines. In fact, we have done very well recently moving southwards to establish new colonies. I really do not know how far we can spread, only time will tell."

"How can you survive for such a long time?"

"We have very few predators mainly because our flesh does not taste too good. Hence, the name 'Fulmar' which means foul Gull. If our nests are threatened, we have a wonderful defence mechanism to keep predators away," she said smugly while puffing up her chest.

"Really? What is that then?"

"Would you like a demonstration?" Chiselton offered.

"Yes!"

Suddenly, a far-reaching jet of green, oily, foul-smelling liquid was discharged from her mouth.

"Wow!" exclaimed Pearl who was cringing and almost choking from the repugnant odour.

"Yes, it is very effective: it sticks to feathers, smells horrible, and it can even prevent a bird from flying. Even Peregrines and Ravens keep their distance as they know if their feathers are clogged with this oil, they cannot fly properly, therefore, destroying their ability to hunt."

"If only we had such an effective weapon! When we are threatened, we flock together and scream loudly but, to be honest, your defence mechanism is so much better! I am invariably harassed by Gulls when I return with food to feed my youngsters, and often, I feel so frightened that I drop the fish to ensure I am not injured. It is extremely frustrating especially after all the work I put in to get the food in the first place!

"Mind you, have you seen the Skuas when they are passing these cliffs? They are the ultimate pirates; not only are they extremely agile, but they are persistent, and whether you are a Tern, Auk or Gull, you have little chance of escaping them with your meal intact. Thankfully, they live much further north than here, so we don't have this constant threat from them. I feel really sorry for the local birds who live near a Skua's nest. However, we are really struggling with the changes in the sea currents. There is just not enough food to maintain our numbers; we have declined by nearly three-quarters over the last 25 years so it's extremely worrying."

"That's a catastrophic drop. This means you are facing the apocalypse* unless things improve very quickly. I quite agree with your opinion of the Skuas; my grandparents used to nest in the vicinity of a pair of Great Skuas and they said life was difficult—perhaps that's why they moved southwards to make their existence a little easier. Have you studied the other birds on these cliffs?" she asked.

"Not really, why?"

"Have you not noticed the strangely shaped eggs of the Razorbills and Guillemots? They are not the normal ovoid form; they are almost triangular in shape: fat at one end tapering to a point at the other."

"Why is that then?"

"Well, as you can see, they are extremely crowded down there on those tiny ledges; there is not enough space to build a nest; thus, the eggs are just laid on the bare rock. The shape of these eggs mean that they just roll in a little circle and, hopefully, do not fall off the cliff. But not only that, those ledges are extremely grubby and many believe that by having a very bulged end to the egg allows enough oxygen to permeate through the shell and keep the embryo alive"

"That's why! I have asked myself that question many times, but I really didn't know the reason. Knowledge is a wonderful thing!"

"There is little point getting older without learning something!" said Chiselton sagaciously*.

"That is so true!" agreed Pearl.

In amongst the Guillemots and Razorbills, there was a constant hubbub of chatter amongst the neighbours. One Guillemot was talking about the risks of being a seagoing hunter.

"I am always afraid of getting coated in oil. I have seen so many getting covered in the stuff and then slowly dying from ingesting the evil concoction* or starving as they cannot fly or hunt. I often have nightmares about it. Do you remember the story about that super tanker which sank off Cornwall many years ago? There were thousands of tonnes of crude oil spilt into the ocean after the Torrey Canyon struck a rocky reef. Man had no idea how to deal with the problem; they used detergents which were worse and more toxic than the crude oil! The whole ecosystem was damaged for decades; the beaches looked clean, but the contamination had wreaked havoc on every living marine creature. It is said that they have improved their techniques and now use a more eco-friendly way of handling oil slicks, but if you are caught in the middle of such a disaster, your chances are very slim.

"I know that the birds 'rescued' from that disaster rarely survived and the 'cleaning process' meant that the birds could not be returned to the sea for many months, as all the waterproofing qualities of their feathers were lost; the majority didn't survive, it took decades for our numbers to recover. I remember my parents telling me that story over and over again," he said with a shrug.

"Yes, I think every bird on this cliff knows the story and perhaps they are more wary nowadays, but I am not so sure. Many still perish in this awful way. One of my recurring nightmares is the day when I had to leave these ledges for the very first time. I still remember vividly that frightening day when my parents flew down and sat on the sea calling me to join them. I flapped my wings, but they were not large enough to carry my weight! I looked around, all the small Guillemot and Razorbill chicks were jumping off the cliff and flopping down on to the sea far below. I swallowed hard, jumped and I was able to glide far enough to miss those deadly rocks below us. I feel a bit sorry for my baby here as he will soon have to do the same. I am amazed that we do it this way. I remember it took a long time for my plumage to grow properly but at least my parents stayed and fed me until I could hunt for myself."

"Yes, I remember that day too; it was an unpleasant experience. What a blessing we can fly now!"

"Absolutely! We wouldn't be able to travel far without our wings although they are not the best. Well, I'd better stretch them now as my wife is getting peckish."

There was a whirl of wings as the Guillemot leapt off the cliff to head out to sea.

A few weeks later, the little auklets made that fateful jump into the unknown to join the others sitting on the choppy seas to begin their marine life, facing the trials of stormy conditions fighting for their survival. The Kittiwake and Fulmar chicks grew and grew, constantly flexing their developing wing muscles until the day they took their maiden flight after which they began to learn the true art of flying. With practice, and a lot of luck, they too, would return to these sheer cliffs to start a family of their own.

As the days shortened, the cliffs began to fall silent. The auks had all departed with their youngsters in tow. The Kittiwakes had also returned to the ocean, so their penetrating *kittiwaak* calls were strangely missing. The rabbit burrows on the cliff tops were now empty; the Puffins had also gone a long way out to sea. Even the Fulmars had flown, but they would be back in late autumn or early spring to claim their territories on the ledges. All the fates of these creatures were dependent on the weather and avoiding any floating oil. A tough life at sea with the mountainous waves and gale force winds but, as their constant return proves, it is possible to succeed in such a harsh environment.

Estuary Echoes

Betwixt land and sea lies a fascinating place
Where mud and slime fight against the currents which here do race
Open land, open skies nowhere a refuge in which to hide
As all the creatures battle with the ever-changing tide
To find a plethora* of food hidden within the salty silt
With beaks probing until their hilt
A vital resource for millions who need
A peaceful place in which to feed
Before flying north to lands beyond the sea,
To a perfect place to raise a family

Farther along the coast, where the high cliffs disappeared, was a large estuary full of oozing mud and pebbly islands. The constant changing tides means that food is available at differing times of the day, and when the tide is full, the birds roost patiently waiting for the mud to reappear. At this time, throngs of birds would rest before feeding up after their long journeys northwards. Many would continue to Iceland, Greenland, Norway and even Siberia. They were looking extremely dapper* with their breeding plumages. Dull, grey winter colours had changed to glowing brick reds or russet browns. Many, excited at the thought of raising young for another year, were getting ready to continue their trek to the barren, chilly tundra areas of Northern Europe.

The estuary is always a battle between the land and sea where the shingle ridges are constantly being eroded and moved along the shore. Many of the banks are stabilised by salt-loving plants whose roots try to bind the ever-shifting stones. Inside the shingle ridges, the mud which had been washed down by the river, has provided a home for innumerable invertebrates, hence, it is irresistible to various wading birds. The relentless movement of water means that it is a very dynamic environment. The estuary is vital for their survival, just like a petrol station is in a very remote area.

The sticky slime is home to millions of tiny creatures, a huge source of protein for the probing bills of various waders. As each species differs in its bill length everyone can access a specific food source. The longest of all, belongs to the Curlew whose bubbling call would soon be heard on the moorland above 'Darcy's' river; it was only a matter of days before he would fly inland to the higher altitudes just a few miles away.

Whimbrel

Next to him was a similar looking bird, a little smaller but with a brown cap and eye stripe, who had just arrived from foreign lands, he was feeding up before his journey northwards.

"Hello, my old friend, you are still here! I thought you would have gone onto the moorlands by now," said Finn the Whimbrel.

"Yes, you are right, I am a little late this year. The early spring was cold and wet, and I didn't feel like going inland into a more hostile habitat, but you are right; it really is time to go. How was your journey northwards?" asked Chester the Curlew.

"Not too bad, but some of the feeding stations are deteriorating or disappearing—the southern estuaries are drying up, and my favourite, the Coto Doñana, is really suffering. Humans have built many hotels nearby, and they are sucking the place dry. I really do not know what will happen to the resident flamingos. Soon, they will not be able to feed. Not only that, but this jewel of the Mediterranean suffered a terrible pollution problem a few years ago as highly-toxic water from a local mine entered the system, killing thousands of insects and birds. They managed to find a solution but it took so many years before the area recovered entirely," replied Finn with a deep sigh.

"That's a disaster, isn't it? I just hope that people wake up to what is happening and do as much as possible to protect the areas which are so important to us. By the way, how long are you staying here?"

"Just a few days and then it's on with my journey: the lure of the north beckons and, as the summer is so short, it's imperative to get there as soon as possible. I hope the snow will have gone by the time I arrive. If I don't see you before I go, I am sure we'll meet up again in a few months' time, and you can tell me all about your summer." remarked Finn.

"Yes, good luck, my friend; stay safe."

Suddenly, a truly remarkable bird alighted nearby. His head and neck were adorned with long flowing red plumes, with accompanying long ear tuffs protruding behind his head; a most amazing sight. "Hi Chester. Not on the moors yet?"

He recognised the voice of Tress from the previous September, but he could not recognise him with all his adornments.

"Wow! What do you look like! I didn't recognise you with all your finery. Last year, you looked rather like a Redshank, what's happened to you?"

"Nothing, this occurs every spring. When I saw you last autumn, all these adornments had been lost. Looks are important, you know! It's the only way I can attract a mate. The competition is fierce, don't you know?" Tress replied rather dismissively.

"Well, I have never seen anything like it! Do all the men have the same ridiculous costume?" Chester wanted to know.

"No, everyone is different; the Ruff can be many colours: black, red and sometimes white, but most ladies prefer the darker colours, I believe. That's why I am called a Ruff!"

"Well I didn't realise that! Do you have a fashion show and then the ladies choose the best looking one?" Chestier assumed.

"In a way, yes, but we all meet up at a traditional site which is in a damp field where the grass is short and then all the males strut around and often fight for the females, who are rather plain, I have to admit. They sit and watch the competitors and then they choose which one would be the best. It can get quite aggressive, I can tell you!"

"I never knew that! All I do is fly in a special way and make my bubbly call, I suppose the female chooses the best displayer and the most vocal. It's all rather civilised. At least I do not have to wear your fancy plumes to get noticed," Chester retorted.

Ruff and Redshank

"You have a point there. It's a bit difficult to fly well with all these extra feathers. However, they don't stay very long. Once the dancing and fighting is over at the lek* and the decisions have been made, then I quickly lose this Ruff. That's why I looked very plain when we met last autumn," Tress explained.

"You can understand why I didn't realise it was you, Tress."

"Of course. Perhaps, if I pass this way next spring, I may have a different look. Don't worry, Chester, I know who you are and so we might not have to do all these introductions all over again!"

"Well, now I am aware of what can happen to you, I won't be so surprised next time."

"I think the meeting will take place soon, so I'd better make my way there. It would be such a waste of energy growing all this stuff and then being too late for the party! Hope to see you in the autumn, and I will tell you all about it." Tress promised.

"I look forward to it. Good luck with the ladies—you really do look extremely exotic."

"Thanks for the compliment, Chester, must rush. Have a good summer. Hopefully, I can see you in a few months." Tress then took to the air and disappeared into the distance.

There was a constant arrival and departure of birds. The estuary was like an airport with domestic and international flights. Chester, was definitely a domestic flight, having only travelled a little distance from his breeding grounds. The newly arrived Sanderlings were resting up after arriving from South Africa, but their stop-over would be brief as they were compelled to leave for Iceland and Siberia—definitely an international flight.

The Sanderlings were running along the shorelines like clockwork toys, chasing the receding waves and then running quickly up the shingle to avoid being swamped by the next. They looked very different: some were still wearing their sparkling white and grey winter plumage whereas others were in their breeding dress with their more sombre, brown backs and russet chests. They were all getting excited about the forthcoming breeding season, and the nervous energy throughout the flock was palpable.*

Nearby, on some concrete blocks, was a small flock of Purple Sandpipers. They had spent the whole winter searching for food amongst the barnacles and seaweed, but they were also getting restless. The call of the north was growing stronger by the day, soon they would be looking for nest sites on the tundra plains of northern Europe, Canada or Greenland.

Purple Sandpiper

A flock of long-legged, long-billed birds landed. They looked superb with their cinnamon chests and heads. Their barred tails and white rumps made them distinctive. These Bar-tailed Godwits were also taking the opportunity to replenish their fat reserves before departing to Iceland where they would raise their broods. Then, in autumn, they take the difficult flight back over the stormy North Atlantic back into Western Europe where their showy brown colouration would be moulted out into subtle greys to mimic the gloomy days of winter.

On one of the pebbly islands, a cat-like call could be heard—a new sound on the estuary. It belonged to a Mediterranean Gull, called Sellsea, who looked extremely handsome with his pure-white wings and black hood punctuated by two small white eyebrows—a true beauty amongst the Gulls. His neighbour, a newly arrived Sandwich Tern, called Smudge, looked up and extended a greeting.

"I have never seen you here before," Smudge commented.

"You wouldn't have because I have just arrived. I thought this place looked an ideal location to set up home; my wife and I agreed we should spend the summer here," answered Sellsea.

"Where were you before?"

"We grew up further south, but the colony was getting a bit cramped, so we thought we should look for pastures new."

"That means your species is expanding its range," deduced Smudge.

"Yes indeed, but it wasn't always that way. In fact, at the beginning of the last century, we were almost facing extinction. Our population was restricted to a small colony in the Black Sea, and things were looking extremely bleak. Our fortunes were saved by some intelligent birds who decided to move away to set up a colony in an entirely different place. Slowly but surely, we spread through the Mediterranean then up through France and eventually, we reached Britain. Since then, we have spread across many areas in the country. We are just continuing this tradition and, if we are successful, I am sure our offspring will look to move into new areas. This strategy has ensured our survival."

"That is an incredible story. It is heartening to hear about a bird which is thriving. We are just maintaining our numbers, but it all depends on the weather. If there are storms at the wrong time, our nests can be washed away which means we have no chicks in that season," replied the Smudge reflectively.

"Yes, we really need a spell of good weather, so we can all thrive. Let's hope we can all do well this year," said the Sellsea optimistically.

The pair was then joined by the diminutive* Little Tern with his bright yellow beak and white forehead. "Morning, folks. I am Tinimo. How are you all?"

"We are fine," the others answered in unison. "We were talking about life in general and how our species are faring*."

"Really? It's always the same problem with us—we just don't seem to produce enough young. Every year it is something! One year, it's the weather; another year, it's a pesky Kestrel; sometimes it's a fox, rat or mouse. Life is such a struggle," Tinimo admitted in an exasperated tone. He then went on to add.

"Have you noticed this fence on this island? The humans have constructed it to keep out the predators which will help us greatly. These semi-circular tubes, well they are mainly for us, so that the chicks can hide under them when we go fishing so the Kestrels or Gulls do not see an easy target. Thus, when the weather is good, we do very well but, as I said before, other years can be terrible. I think we all need a good season."

"That's all we want, my little friend," they both said.

In the channel close by, the *keeyaw* cry of a Common Tern could be heard, and behind him, a very similar bird but with a pale-blue tinted breast, was an Arctic Tern. Tinimo spoke to the other two and said, "Do you see that second bird? He is one of the longest fliers in the world; each year, they fly from pole to pole, spending the northern winter near the Antarctic, with some of them returning to summer in the Arctic. I thought it was bad enough to fly to the coasts off central Africa but to continue farther—well, that really is an achievement."

"It's incredible what some species have to do to make a living," said Sellsea, who was well aware that his wanderings were puny* in comparison to others.

"I was chatting to him earlier and he was telling me that there are grave problems in the Antarctic: the warming climate is breaking up the ice sheets, making it impossible for some species to gather enough food. He informed me that only a couple of young fledged this year from a huge Adele penguin colony numbering thousands of pairs—what a catastrophic season! It seems that the ice floes* had been washed into their bay and the birds had difficulties getting to the sea. How long can they survive if they continue to face such adversity?" explained Tinimo poignantly with a tear dribbling down his face.

The others just stared in disbelief, unable to utter a response. They knew they had a few problems, but to hear of such dreadful news from the Southern Hemisphere made them realise that there is a global crisis and they are merely innocent victims awaiting their fate. Perhaps, the recent unpredictable weather with gales, heavy downpours and droughts were just a reflection and indication of the inevitable* changes they would all have to face.

An image of white beauty alighted beside the edge of the channel and began to hunt for fish. His long, black legs and long neck meant he could hunt well not only in the shallows but in the deeper waters too. The Egret looked beautiful with long, delicate plumes adorning his back. He looked up at the trio of birds and said hello.

Little Egret

"Good weather for fishing," said the Terns.

"Not bad I suppose," replied the Egret.

"Why don't you nest here on the island like the rest of us?"

"No, we like to build a fairly substantial nest to keep our young out of harm's way. We think it's too risky on the ground, so we nest together in a colony in trees, usually alongside Herons who look very menacing to other birds and animals."

"You haven't been on this estuary for very long, have you?" asked Tinimo.

"You are an extremely observant little bird; no, we are newcomers to this country. Haven't you noticed that the climate is changing? We were once confined to Southern Europe and like you, Mr Mediterranean Gull, we have moved steadily northwards to find the ideal conditions to breed. Other southern Herons: the Great White Egret, Cattle Egret, Purple Heron, Little Bittern and Night Heron have also followed our example and have just begun to breed here too. It's a clear sign that things are changing.

"Our species has had a very chequered history. We were hunted mercilessly in the nineteenth century, along with the Great Crested Grebe, because of our fine feathers. Ladies thought it very fashionable to have our plumes in their hats! Just imagine how many of us died in the name of fashion! Our saviour was a group of women, who at the end of the nineteenth century, thought it was rather barbaric, and so they formed a society to ban cruelty towards birds. They ensured that wild birds should not provide a fashionable accessory to the millinery* trade. This was the beginning of the RSPB (the Royal Society for the Protection of Birds), one of the largest conservation groups in the world today with over one million members, so I suppose the sacrifices made by my ancestors have had a huge positive effect for us all today. The fences and anti-predator measures taken here on this little pebble island were probably undertaken by this organisation—so, at last, hopefully, we can look forward to a better future!"

"We didn't know that," said the trio. "Respect, brother!"

"Well, I can't stand around here, idly chatting away. There are fish to be caught, and the lady at home wants to stretch her wings and legs, so I'd better get down to some serious fishing before I take over the domestic duties!" He then wandered off into the water, made a few jabs, picked up a few silvery fish and then flew off towards a distant clump of trees, which was obviously where the Heronry was.

Suddenly, chaos spread across the whole area: flocks of birds took to the air, wheeling around in sheer panic. A large raptor, with a dark brown back and brilliant white underparts, slowly made its way over the estuary. He started to circle then, suddenly, folded his wings and plunged into the water feet first with a large splash. A few seconds later, the bird reappeared and, with a lot of effort, managed to get airborne. It was hardly surprising that it was difficult as the bird had a large fish in his talons. He skimmed across the water, landed on a jetty and began to devour his meal.

Osprey

"Wow! Did you see that?" asked the Smudge to his neighbour.

"Pretty impressive stuff, I must admit," replied Tinimo.

"The Osprey is on his way northwards, he obviously needed a bite to eat. He's a bit late this year, as he is normally here in early April; perhaps the winds were not too favourable this year." Smudge explained.

"How long is his journey?"

"Well, he spends the winter in West Africa, so it is a long way. I really do not understand why he travels so far as there is always a lot of fish here, even in mid-winter. Perhaps he just does not have enough fat to keep out the icy winds?"

"That's an interesting idea, but who knows?"

"He'll probably stay a few days before carrying on northwards. A handsome bird and a real threat to any large fish here. He'll be back in the autumn for a few days to have a feast on his return trip. He always brings a bit of excitement to the estuary and always causes a lot of panic!" admitted Smudge.

The ever-changing comings and goings meant that the estuary was always an interesting place, but by mid-May, most of the waders had left for their breeding grounds, leaving just the Terns and Gulls to raise their broods. However, by mid-July, many waders would start returning, including the youngsters, before some of them would continue on their long journey southwards. This 'airport' always had a lot going on.

As the weeks passed, the Terns and Gulls on the pebbly island were busy raising their families and the constant noise increased appreciably as the young begged loudly for food. Their maiden flights were always accompanied by excited cries from their parents and others. Once the youngsters had mastered their flying skills, there was a sense of urgency from the migratory species; their task had been achieved and the urge to move southwards was becoming ever stronger. Soon it would be time to leave these shores and the familiar, raucous Tern calls would become just a memory.

As the summer comes to an end, there is an influx of old faces: the returning waders, some now clad in more sombre dress, accompanied by their new offspring, take up a brief residence.

Chester had just returned to his winter grounds on the estuary and he was pleased to see his friend Finn, the Whimbrel.

"Hey, Finn, you are back! Great to see you again. How are things?"

"Fine. May I introduce you to my children? Here are Willis and Willow; I am pleased to say they have arrived here safe and sound," replied Finn.

"So, you had a good summer then!"

"Well, two of my offspring survived but the other two did not, that's the way it goes."

"Why, what happened?"

"Well, the tundra is a harsh environment, there are a lot of predators which you do not have here: Snowy Owls, Gyr Falcons Polar bears and Arctic foxes. They are all looking for an easy meal."

"What's a Gyr Falcon?" asked Chester.

Gyr Falcon

"Well, you are very familiar with a Peregrine; just add a few inches here and there, and you have some idea what they are like! They can fell a large Goose, so they are a real threat to all. Many are pure white with the odd black spot on the breast, others are grey, but it doesn't matter what colour they are, because their power and incredible hunting skills are the same."

"I am sure they are formidable creatures," replied Chester.

"Anyway, things started well, the four eggs hatched on time, but once the youngsters were a little more mobile, a Snowy Owl noticed one moving around, despite my warning cries to stay still. Unfortunately, the owl's keen eyesight meant he had no chance. From that moment, the other three always heeded my warnings and they all grew to the flying stage," explained Finn.

"Just before we decided to migrate southwards, we were startled by a white Gyr Falcon and, despite flying as well as we could, another youngster was caught. We didn't stay much longer and began our long trek southwards. We have just arrived and will rest up a bit before moving on southwards."

"That's a terribly sad story but at least you raised two lovely children; you should be proud," said Chester.

"You are right. I should be grateful for what I have. Anyway, if we don't meet up again, I hope you have a good winter and perhaps we will meet up in the spring. Good luck my friend."

"You too."

Curlew

Chester was eagerly awaiting the return of Tress, the Ruff, but in vain. Perhaps the weather systems had altered his migration route, or something had happened to him. Chester would have to sit out a cold winter to see if he returned the following spring with his new adornments. Only time would tell.

The Osprey, accompanied by a youngster, spent a leisurely week hunting mullet before moving on. The Common Gulls returned and slowly lived up to their name by building up their numbers. They would spend the autumn and winter feeding on the beaches or fields looking for tasty morsels.

Finally, the October chills bring the return of the vast duck flocks; the whistling Wigeon, the peeping Teal, the croaking Brent Geese and the whooping Whooper Swans. The constant wheeling flocks of waders and ducks show that this place is really their haven. This huge food source encourages the predators, including the Peregrine, to spend the winter here as well. Here the ducks, geese and waders will face the icy blasts of the forthcoming season waiting until the days begin to lengthen when the urge to breed makes them decide to move northwards to find their true homeland once again.

Reed-Bed Ramblings

A sea of swaying feathered-topped reeds
Rustling in the breeze
Home to many with their specialist needs
The booming Bittern, the Bearded Tit
The whistling otter, part of a community, so closely knit

On to the edge of the estuary stood a large marsh with a sizeable phragmites reed bed, and during the early spring, it reverberated* to a loud boom emanating* from the depths of the vegetation. The source of this sound was a Bittern who wrenched his body in a peculiar way to force this sound out of the depths of his very being. A Moorhen, walking nearby, was rather surprised to see the exertion needed to produce such a thunderous noise.

"That looks hard work to me," she uttered.

The large, brown, Bittern stared down at her and decided to take some time out and speak to her. "Yes, it is not easy but at least I know that if there are any females around, they will have no excuse not to hear me!" explained Byron.

"You can say that again. It's almost deafening, my ears are still ringing! This is the first time I have heard it. Have you just found your voice this year?"

"No, I have always had this loud voice, but this is the first time I have been here in spring, I think it would be the perfect place to set up home," answered Byron.

"Have you just arrived?" inquired the moorhen.

"No, I arrived in the late autumn, life has been fairly easy here: there are a lot of fish and eels on offer, so there is plenty to eat. Now that spring is here, there will be loads of frogs and toads to keep me well fed as well! Life looks rosy."

"Where were you before, then?"

"I was born on a marsh some miles away, but there were too many birds; in the end, I decided to seek my fortune elsewhere."

"That means you are a very successful species, then."

"Oh, far from it! Many years ago, before mass drainage took place in this country, we were a familiar species, but as the habitat disappeared, so did we. Not so long ago we were down to single figures in this country, and the future looked extremely bleak. We were clinging on for survival, and extinction was threatening." replied Byron in a sad voice.

"What brought you back from the brink?"

"Unusually, man intervened and realised our plight, and, following extensive studies, they worked out our specific requirements. They took everything into consideration such as the depth of the water, the number of hidden shorelines and the quality of the reeds to create some perfect habitats for us to be successful. There have been numerous massive projects to increase marshlands for us, tailored for our special needs, naturally, we have responded. From a few 'booming' males, we now have exceeded the magic 100 mark, and if things continue the way they are, who knows how many there will be in the future? These massive changes have benefited other species too.

"The Marsh Harrier was also down to a couple of pairs but since the renovation projects and new habitat creation, they are now thriving. Not only that, otters are becoming increasingly common in these new haunts as well. Life is looking better for so many creatures, and I am living proof that, when the right steps are taken, we can all pull back from the abyss," said Byron rather triumphantly.

"I am so pleased to hear a good luck story. I must admit there does seem to be more life in the reeds nowadays. I often hear the pinging of the Bearded Tits—that's another species which seems to be thriving. Obviously, your stories are closely intertwined."

"You are absolutely correct—the specialised reed-loving species are doing well nowadays. It is amazing what can be achieved in a few years with the help of experienced ecologists who know what we crave."

"Well, I'd better let you get back to your booming as perhaps a female is listening out for your diagnostic call."

"You never know."

By late April, there was a cacophony* of sound from the newly-arrived Sedge and Reed Warblers. Both species were working hard to construct their beautifully-woven nests from the reeds. A female Reed Warbler looked over at her neighbour giving her a smile. "Let's hope we have a good year."

Sedge Warbler

"Yes. Mind you, last year was peculiar," replied her neighbour.

"Why is that?"

"Well I seem to remember laying four eggs, which I kept warm for a few weeks or so, and then they all hatched. I was delighted, needless to say. As I was feeling a bit peckish, and I knew it was mild enough to keep the fledglings warm, I went out for a bite to eat, but when I returned, there was just one hatchling left. My husband and I kept him warm and fed him as usual but he had such an appetite; no matter how much we brought him, he was screaming for more. I have never seen a young bird eat so much in my life! It was exhausting for us both. Soon, he was a giant and his feathers began to grow but they were not brown like mine, they were black and white. I really didn't know what to make of it. Soon, he was bigger than the whole nest and I ended up standing on his back to give him his dinner! In the end, he was quite chubby and twice my height; he was a truly funny looking thing. One day, he just spread his wings and flew away. I really don't know what to make of it."

"I think another bird played a trick on you. It was a Cuckoo; they prey on unsuspecting birds to bring up their babies. It seems you left the nest at exactly the wrong time, and she took that opportunity to lay her egg. Not only are they very surreptitious* but also extremely clever, you know. Perhaps this year, you will be more vigilant to ensure that you bring up your own children rather than being a foster parent. As you said, it was really hard work, not surprising, looking at the size of the adult. I think we should be more careful this year, don't you?"

"Yes, you are so right."

An explosive call made them both jump.

"Must you be so loud?" said the Reed Warbler to the plain brown Warbler hopping nearby.

"Sorry about that," replied Bramble, the Cetti's Warbler, "it's just the way we are. Everyone else makes such a din that we have turned up the volume to make sure we are heard."

"How was your migration?" asked the Reed Warbler.

"Migration? We do not migrate! We are the only wetland Warbler to stay here throughout the winter; we are pretty tough, as you can imagine," replied Bramble.

"So, have you always lived here?"

"Actually, no. We arrived in the 1970s and have managed to hang on ever since. In a mild winter, when we do well we can spread to new areas but, then again, in a bad one, we suffer a high mortality rate and disappear from some places. However, the recent winters have been fairly mild, so we are doing all right."

"That's great news. If only I didn't have to travel so far! There are some advantages to not migrating, I suppose. *Tempus fugit* (time flies) so I'd better get back to my nest building!"

Bramble hopped through the reeds when he met up with a familiar friend: Rustin, the Bearded Tit. He looked very refined with his black, droopy moustache, grey head, piercing yellow eyes and long graduated tail.

"Hello, Rustin. Busy?"

"Yes, I am enjoying some insects; they taste so much better than seeds!"

"How do you know?"

"Well, because I eat both. In spring and summer, I feast on insects whereas in winter, I have to make do with seeds. It may sound odd, but my intestines change in the autumn as the insect life dwindles. I believe they double in length so that my body can cope with eating just seeds; it is a clever adaptation which allows me to stay in the reed bed throughout the year. It does save a lot of migrating too!"

Bearded Tit

"That's very interesting. I find the winter really tough, as I depend on finding insects the whole year round. You really do have a superior strategy to see you through!"

"Well, we are also lucky that humans have expanded the wetland areas allowing new reed beds to develop, which means we have more places to live. Not only that, but some people have actually built us ready-made nests which saves us a lot of work! They even provide grit trays in the winter," replied Rustin.

"Grit trays? What's that?"

"Well, you remember I told you that we change our diet in the winter and eat only seeds; they do play havoc with the old digestive system, but if we eat a little grit, it helps to grind down the seeds allowing us to get the maximum nutrients from them. A little roughage is always a good thing."

"That's good to know. I am so happy that people are helping you to expand your range; it's always encouraging to hear a positive story. Anyway, I'd better be getting on, there is so much to do."

Rustin agreed, and he flew off, emitting his characteristic *ping ping* call. This sound would remain in the reed-bed throughout the year, especially on calm sunny days even in the depths of winter. But the Warblers would depart in the autumn, leaving just the hardy species to survive the winter. The marsh population of Bitterns would probably be boosted by birds escaping the rigours of a European winter, but their crepuscular* habits and cryptic plumage would mean very few humans would actually realise they were around. A truly unobtrusive creature whose presence would be proclaimed once they started booming again in the spring.

Moorland Muses

Shrouded in cloud on a gloomy day,
The mountain tops forever grey
Is a world so misunderstood, where creatures survive
The bitterest of days, living side by side
The predator and prey, a constant chase
Over endless moorland without a face
But here in summer, when the sun's rays break through, reveals an
astounding place
Of desolate beauty and grace to make anyone's pulse race.

Finally, Chester the Curlew took off from the estuary and headed inland to the purple heather-clad moors to begin his bubbling display calls. The desolate landscape provided a haven for him and others. A mournful*, melodic song emanated from a scree* slope at the bottom of a small cliff, where a Ring Ouzel sat there singing away. His white breast band shone out like a beacon—such a beautiful Blackbird, his melancholic melodies were perfect for the mood of these windswept uplands.

Autumn-plumaged Ring Ouzel

The whole area was boggy with deep peat formed over generations: an ideal place for a Curlew whose long down-curved beak could find enough invertebrate life to sustain him and his future brood. The cotton grass and sphagnum moss showed just how saturated the earth is. Some of the moorland contained 'feather beds,' a place which trembles underfoot, a web of dank vegetation and sphagnum moss floating on an underground lake—a very dangerous place for unwary humans to wander.

Curlew

Looking around, the Curlew could breathe in the whole atmosphere of this very special place, a remote area where the impact of man was not very discernible. The harsh climate ensured that farming could not be performed at these higher elevations: apart from a few wild ponies and a few scraggy sheep, he and his family were basically alone. Only the heather with its purple blooms brought some colour to this area which was often shrouded in low-level cloud, adding to the haunting feeling that this place has. A pair of Golden Plovers also brought a touch of brightness with their gold-spangled* backs and black fronts; they eked out a living by looking for insects in the wet bog lands, their plaintive calls absolutely in keeping with the wild scenery.

Another highland songster was the diminutive* Whinchat who stood on a dwarf tree and also let rip with his melancholic song. His beige-pink breast and spangled back, a combination of beige and browns, was a subtle camouflage against the various hues of the moor. However, his most stunning feature was his white eyebrow and black eye-stripe, giving him a rather distinguished look. His return to the moor every late April brought yet another song to this endless scenery. Chester also watched a Meadow Pipit ascend into the sky and then parachute back down to earth with his distinctive trilling song.

Whinchat, in its more subdued autumn plumage

In the distance, he could hear the Red Grouse calling to each other, and he knew that, in the late summer, a human invasion would take place ending the peace and solitude which would be broken by the incessant cries of the beaters as they frightened the Grouse towards the awaiting guns. The 'Glorious Twelfth', (of August), a real misnomer, was the opening day of the hunting season when the massacre would begin. It was a sign that even these remoter regions could bear witness to the senseless killing of such a very special bird—the only endemic* species in Britain. He knew that this 'natural' landscape was manufactured for hunters and their poor quarry*: the Grouse.

Chester had heard stories that on some moorlands, unscrupulous* game keepers had laid traps and poisons to kill any predators who had a liking for Grouse meat resulting in many protected birds such as Eagles, Kites, Buzzards and Falcons being eradicated from these areas; such a sad indictment of the hunting business. It had been said that laws had been passed to protect every species, but away from prying eyes, these deeds are still continuing. He had not noticed any extra activities over the last few years, but he was aware that both the Hen Harrier and Merlin had become a rarity. He missed the dynamic sky dancing of the male Hen Harrier whose ghost-like grey plumage and black wingtips provided a wonderful spectacle.

Female Hen Harrier

He knew that this species was a threat to him and his brood, but, even so, the moor was just not the same without him.

Overhead, there was a sudden *kikakikabrrrup* sound and Chester recognised his friend, the Snipe, who was showing off, trying to impress the ladies. The drumming sound was something special, not made by calling, but by his reverberating* tail feathers which produced this amazing sound—a grasshopper of a bird! The Snipe would call and then head into a dive; the speed and the special alignment of his outer tail feathers would make them tremble and produce this wildest of sounds—a perfect example of sound replicating the environment.

Snipe

On the edge of the moorland, close to the silver birches where the Redstarts sing merrily, is a special place: the grass is short and trampled, and every year, one of nature's spectacular events takes place. The morning twilight of early spring echoes to the sound of the bubbling and squealing Black Grouse. The evocative* call raises the hairs of even the most impassive of observers. The males with flame-red eyebrows, clad in black with a lyre-shaped tail and white bottoms, meet at this lek to perform their amazing dances, moving backwards and forwards, feigning* a fight. This ballet lasts for a few hours, and the tawdry females look on impassively, waiting to see who the dominant male was, as he would pass on the best genes for the next generation.

"Which one do you think is the best, Carly?"

"Well, that one on the left has the best looks and he does have a lovely tone to his voice, he also seems to be the strongest, the other males do seem to be somewhat afraid of him. Yes, I think he is the one."

"But the one at the back is also cute!" replied Tess. "But, then again, does it matter? The moment the nest is built and we are sitting on eggs, we never see them again! At least our chicks are mobile almost immediately after they hatch, and all we have to do is teach them how to recognise the best food!"

"Don't forget we also have to try to protect them from the local crows and other predators; sometimes, it is a futile exercise as some are much stronger than we are, but we usually manage to get a few fledged," Carly admitted.

"Yes, we usually do, but have you seen some of the other birds where the parents spend every daylight hour searching for food to keep their little ones alive—that must be really exhausting! I think we have a much easier life, but it's hard work looking for enough to eat. At least, the bilberries and blueberries are in season when the chicks reach their most demanding stage. I remember my first snow-bound winter was really difficult; as I spent all day digging away, trying to find seeds and berries under the snow. That experience taught me how to survive."

"I remember that too. If our kids get through that difficult phase, then they'll be just fine. Those short days with the baying Red Deer rutting and the clash of antlers sending shivers through my whole body as the whole landscape reverberates with that violent sound."

"Yes, it really is a tough battle, and many of the contenders are mortally wounded in their fight to be lord of the moors. I know that clash will ensue once the new antlers are grown and the frosts and snows arrive. It won't be long now before the young fawns are born, with their mothers tending them throughout the summer."

The bubbling of the blackcock subsided, and as the two black hens looked towards the 'dance floor', it was now deserted.

"I think the show is over, so let's get back into the trees to see if we can find something juicy to eat."

As the sun gained in strength, the morning mists continued to rise eerily from the valley bottom, the remaining birds disappeared into the trees, ready for the show to be repeated the following day.

Once the long days of summer are over and families raised, certain birds leave the ever-toughening conditions of the high moorlands. The Ring Ouzel, Whinchat and Wheatear would leave the country, the Curlew, Snipe and Meadow Pipit would descend to the coast for the warmer conditions. Meanwhile, the Red and Black Grouse would stay through the icy grips of winter and, as most people are loathe to enter this remote and unwelcoming landscape at this time of year, these birds can at last enjoy the solitude of this wildest of habitats.

Moorland scene

Northern Lights

As the blackness of winter wanes
Comes an awakening which gradually gains
In strength and welcomes all flying creatures from afar
To set home on wind-swept slopes and verdant machair*
To fill this habitat with trilling songs in the air

High up in the northern isles of Scotland is another gem. Endless summer days with twilight replacing the blackness of the long winter evenings. An area colourful in spring with the machair* resplendent in a multitude of colourful flowers and amongst this distinctive vegetation a few endearing creatures who thrive in this wind-swept landscape.

Spinning around like a top on a small lochan* was a female Red-necked Phalarope—a stunning beauty amongst the wading birds. Her dark grey back and head contrasted with her white throat and, as the name implies, the beautiful orangey-red neck patch. She was picking daintily at the surface of the water collecting the emerging insects. This is a time of plenty and therefore, she was feeding up eagerly after her long migration northwards from the seas off Africa.

Unlike other waders, these enchanting birds swim using their knobbly toes, (Grebes, Moorhens and Coots have the same adaption), to propel them through the water. Another interesting fact about this special group of three waders, (Red-necked, Grey and Wilson's) is that the females are larger and far more colourful than their male counterparts. These Phalaropes exhibit role reversal: the females display to the males, lay their eggs and then abandon their young.

Red-necked Phalarope

Suddenly, the first bird was joined by another equally beautiful female.

"Hello, Candice. Oh, I am so pleased you are back! I was getting a bit lonely here." She gave her a broad smile.

"Yes, I have just turned up—I am thrilled to be home. Have you seen any suitors* yet?"

"No, actually I haven't. Don't worry, they will be here any time soon," replied Sienna.

"How many husbands did you have last year?"

"A couple, and they did a good job: most of the babies were raised so I am quite pleased with my choices. Perhaps, I might do the same this year as I know those two can be trusted with all the domestic duties. How about you?"

"Well, I had a couple too but one of them was a disappointment. I don't think he really had his heart in it, whether it was neglect or misfortune, he completely failed to raise any of my children. Needless to say, I won't pick him again!"

The birds looked around and they could see a Red-throated Diver already incubating eggs on her nest built beside the edge of the loch. As these birds are so ungainly* on land, they always choose to nest right on the edge of the water so they can slip away without trying to walk first. Her partner was actively fishing at the other end of the pool.

They were absolutely no threat to the two exquisite Phalaropes.

On these desolate islands, other birds had moved in for the summer to utilise the endless hours of daylight to the fullest. On the higher moorland, were the returning Curlews and Whimbrels whose distinctive display calls drifted across the barren landscape. In the wetter areas, tiny Dunlins in their summer livery* also choose this area to breed.

Offshore and on the cliff faces were a multitude of auks including the Black Guillemot, who needs cooler waters in which to hunt. The northern seas abound with fish and hence, the huge Gannet colonies here in these northern outposts of the country. However, the seabird predators have also set up home on the moorlands nearby. Both Arctic and Great Skuas are found here and they defend their territories extremely aggressively, bombarding any intruder, including man, should they be foolhardy enough to encroach onto 'their' land.

The largest and most regal* of all the predators is the White-tailed Eagle whose sheer size dominates the skies. His massive, fingered-wings and pure white tail make him a wonder to behold. Mercifully, for most, his favourite prey is fish and he is often seen patrolling the lochs and inlets causing panic wherever he goes. Another fish hunter is the otter whose whistling calls can be heard from both the shoreline and the lochans. There is enough food to sustain a healthy otter population.

Once spring arrives, a new grating sound can be heard emanating from the long grasses. The crrrk, crrrk almost like a wooden comb being plucked shows that the retiring* Corncrake has managed its massive migration back to the islands. This species was once widespread throughout the UK but with mechanisation and pesticides it has been reduced to a rump* population, far away from the intensively farmed areas.

The crofters* have also taken major steps to allow this bird to thrive by altering their harvesting technique so that the young birds can escape to safety when the crops are being brought in. It is a sad indictment* to modern farm practices that Corncrakes are restricted to the most unfavourable areas of the country. This reclusive* bird shuns mankind and only here on these islands, can they find the peace and solitude they crave.

Meanwhile, back on the little lochan, a few new arrivals had appeared and now there was a small flock of Red-necked Phalaropes including a few smaller males. Both Candice and Sienna went out to greet the newcomers. They began to show off their bright colours and beauty trying to entice a male to commit himself to a summer of total parenthood.

Candice did beguile* a certain male and, as he said he was willing to look after her children, they then sought out the best place to build their moss-filled nest amongst the grassy tussocks. Here, the male would incubate the eggs until they hatched, he would then teach the chicks how to feed on the local pools. Fortunately for him, Phalarope chicks are almost immediately mobile once their fluffy down dries and so they soon become self-reliant, but he still needs to warn them of any impending danger.

Candice, on the other hand, would have probably laid a second clutch of eggs with another male being given the task of bringing up her other brood. Sienna, on a nearby loch did exactly the same—an ingenious way to double the number of chicks produced during the short breeding season in the Northern Isles.

Once the nights begin to draw in, the insectivorous species flee southwards to avoid the chill and the cloak of darkness. Sometimes in late autumn, the northern night skies are illuminated with vibrant colours from the aurora borealis emanating from the polar regions. That hostile environment is closing down for winter and only the specialist creatures adapted to polar life can survive the winter's onslaught.

Heathland Haunts

Rising mist above a purple scene of heather
The gorse, ferns, and the odd sparse tree
A world of animals and birds often hard to see
Special creatures adapted to the sandy terrain,
The stubby-taloned Buzzard who raids wasp nests'
Again, and again
Eerie calls echo during the dead of night
Ghost-like owls on silent wings in flight
Mean that we have to protect the heaths with all our might

Barn Owl

Further south, and at much lower altitudes, are the lowland heaths—a product of geology, where sandstone predominates and the indigenous* plant life struggles to find nutrients. Despite the sandy soils not being very fertile, owing to their high acid levels, many unusual plants thrive here. In fact, in some boggy areas, there are so few nutrients that some plants have had to find their own source and one, in particular, compensates by catching its own insects to make up the shortfall. The aptly-named Sundew adorns the summer bogs as they sparkle like dew in the sunlight. However, the crystal droplets adorning each tentacle is a sticky trap for any tiny insect attracted to the red centre of the 'flower' The unfortunate victims are ingested. This brilliant adaptation has allowed this tiny plant to survive in the most inhospitable areas of the marshy areas.

The winter moon shone down on the frosty heath and very little was moving, save for the eerie ghost-like figure of a Barn Owl. His silent wingbeats and moth-like movements ensured his superb hearing skills would pick up the quietest of rustles amongst the dank* grass covering the heath. It is a tough time for this crepuscular* creature: the low temperatures and chilling winds means he needs to find food before sunrise to sustain him through another day.

This most beautiful of owls is probably more suited to warmer climates, and indeed, it is one of the few birds which is found on every continent of the world. The chilly British winter means that they have to struggle through the cold months but, somehow, they cling on. They bring joy to everyone who has the pleasure of seeing them except, of course, the mice on which they prey!

As the tardy* sun rises on this landscape, many things become discernible*: the rolling terrain with its covering of heather and gorse, dank grasslands beside gurgling brooks, and invasive silver birches on the edge of the woodlands. Unlike the upland moors, this is a less harsh habitat, allowing many species to thrive. Lowland birds are more common but also there are the true heathland creatures which are found nowhere else. The sandy soils allow rare reptiles to make their living, but they are, naturally, nowhere to be found during the winter.

The crisp air of winter is not totally devoid of sound. A rasping call is emitted from a gorse bush and then, suddenly, in all its splendour, a Dartford Warbler pops out onto the highest twig. His exquisite purple breast and brown back makes him a heathland beauty—his colouration matches the heather perfectly. His long tail means he resembles a lollipop as he flies from bush to bush in search of things to eat. This tiny Warbler is the only true resident of its family and, unlike all the other Warblers who migrate to survive, he has the difficult task of coping with the unpredictable British winter.

Dartford Warbler

During a particularly harsh winter the gorse bushes and heather are frozen solid it is the death knell for the local population. However, the tough little creatures who survive will then compensate the following summer by having two broods to ensure that their numbers recover sufficiently to return to their former haunts. It's a high risk strategy but, evidently, it is successful.

The Dartford Warbler is assisted in its survival by another bird whose observation skills he uses to warn him of danger is the Stonechat. It is a stunning ball-like bird with an orange breast, black head, white collar and white wing flashes, he seems to have the role of the observer. His constant *chat, chat* call means the Dartford Warbler knows exactly where he is, and that his 'guardian angel' is watching over him. Both birds are similar in character: both are a bundle of nerves, constantly on the move and always very alert. There seems to be an almost symbiotic* relationship between them.

"Good day, Pebble, my handsome friend," said the Dartford Warbler. "Looks like it's going to be a fine day, at last."

"Yes, Georgie, you are right, these short winter days don't allow us much time to find something to eat, do they? Once this frost disappears, we should be able to collect enough today."

"It really is tough out here. When the icy wind blows, there is no chance of perching up and surveying the landscape, is there?" stated Georgie in a resigned way.

Stonechat

"No, there isn't but somehow I always do, it's just my nature; I need to know what is going on. There are a few predators around, I don't want to be caught napping! Are you aware of that long-tailed grey and white bird with the bandit mask? It's a Great Grey Shrike, a rather dangerous neighbour. They sit up on top of a bush and closely observe everything, then suddenly, they swoop down to catch their prey, be it an insect or some unfortunate bird. They like these thorn bushes as they sometimes impale their victims on the spikes! That's why they are called the butcher bird— their favourite bush may be covered with the cadavers of his 'successes'. I am keeping my eye on him, always making sure there is a big distance between us!" explained Pebble.

"I know you are extremely vigilant, and I do appreciate your efforts; it is so reassuring to have you around!"

The two were interrupted when a short-tailed pale brown Lark took to the air and began his fluttering song flight. A rich descending warble with such pure clarity filled the air, *pijueejuee,* the haunting yet uplifting song of the Woodlark. Although breeding would not take place for weeks to come, this bird uses the fine winter days to show others that it is his territory and that no unwelcome guests are wanted.

The winter months drag on, as the small creatures use every opportunity to find food. Sometimes, flocks of Winter Thrushes arrive to find sustenance amongst the trees and bushes. The conifers offer Crossbills their cones on which they feast, soon they will be building their nests to utilise the tree's seed crop in early spring.

Spring is heralded by new arrivals, the Curlews who haunt the boggy areas proclaim their presence by their bubbling display flights, the Woodlark goes into overdrive with his melodic song flight, and both the Stonechat and Dartford Warbler sing in earnest. With the warming days, the reptiles awaken from their hibernation: adders warm themselves on sunny banks and the true heathland specialities, the Sand Lizard and Smooth Snake, also emerge to hunt and find a partner.

In early May, Pebble was singing on top of his favourite gorse bush when he suddenly noticed something strange amongst the bracken and ferns below him—it looked like a piece of wood, but he had never noticed it before. Suddenly, the piece of 'wood' yawned with a massive gape and opened two huge black eyes!

Nightjar

"Wow! I hardly noticed you there with your cryptic* camouflage," said Pebble, somewhat startled.

"That's the whole point," said the peculiar bird. "I do not want to be seen! I spend the whole day resting before I start hunting at night. Have you not thought about the birds which nest on the ground? They are usually dull in their plumage so that they can remain hidden. You are extremely showy with your orange, black and white but you nest in thorny bushes which afford you protection. I do not have that; therefore, my subtle tones of browns, greys and stripes ensure I can fool most creatures and remain safe during the daylight hours. At night, I have few threats as I am an agile flier which allows me to catch insects. The long whiskers around my mouth assist me in this task."

"Do you know, I have never thought about ground nesting birds before, but you are right. Wait a minute! What about the Pheasant? That is a really brightly coloured bird and they nest on the ground!" said Pebble somewhat triumphantly.

"Good point, but the female is dull, which supports my argument, you may have forgotten this bird is not an indigenous* species; it was introduced from China where it spends its time hidden in rhododendron undergrowth and it is quite secretive. It obviously has changed its habits and character since it arrived in Europe!"

"I didn't realise it is not a native bird, yes, I have to admit the female is rather boring in its colouration. I must say I haven't noticed you before; have you just arrived?"

"I have been back a few days, if you must know. A few weeks ago, I was in the heat of Africa, but I am here for the summer," replied Noel the Nightjar.

"Why do you arrive much later than the other migrants? Some have been back for over a month."

"Well, I need the warm evenings to hunt my prey so there is little point coming any earlier."

"What could you possibly hunt at night?"

"Moths" was Noel's curt reply.

"What! Are there enough to feed a big bird like you?"

"Obviously. But we are very dependent on the weather; we really need warm, dry nights to get enough of them. It is a risky business coming to this country, but we are still hanging on."

"By the way, as you are up all night, have you noticed that strange *churring* noise? It has only recently started, but it's very eerie and haunting, you know," Pebble pointed out.

"That's me!" Noel chuckled. "I *churr* for hours to attract a mate. I also fly around clapping my wings to show off my large white patches just to make sure she notices me!"

"So, it's you! I had no idea that a bird could make such a peculiar noise."

"Yes, I know. Humans have invented many stories about us as we are nocturnal and have such an unusual call. They have given us so many strange names, some even believed we drank milk from goats at night! Hence, our name the 'goatsucker'. In the past, people knew nothing about us; we became part of rural folklore. Fortunately, some have realised how special we are and have worked tirelessly to maintain our habitat. We have rewarded their efforts by returning to many rejuvenated sites. However, we really are on the north-western edge of our range, who knows, if the summers become warmer and drier, we may expand, but on the other hand, if the weather deteriorates, we may have to retreat to better climates," Noel added.

"Really? It would be a great shame to lose your wonderful 'song'. It really brings a sense of magic to this landscape. I hope we have a lot of fine nights and you can thrive."

"That really would be a blessing."

That evening, as Pebble was hiding amongst the prickly gorse, he decided to stay awake a bit longer and, sure enough, just after sunset, the Nightjar flew up silently from the bracken and headed towards a single pine tree. The white 'headlights' in his wings shining brightly in the gathering gloom. As he flew, he emitted a *guuik* call which added to the atmosphere. Once he had settled along a branch, he began to *churr,* a mechanical-like sound, varying in pitch and volume, a really idiosyncratic* noise.

The Nightjar was not the only crepuscular* 'songster'. The powerful song of a Nightingale drifted across the open heath from a nearby copse—its tones and variations a beauty to hear.

Above the woodland, a silhouette of a fat, long-billed wader appeared with stiff, quivering wings as it passed slowly over the edge of the nearby woodland. It made a strange *psst* call followed by a frog-like croak as it continued its pedestrian flight across the edge of its territory. Pebble was fascinated by the strange antics of the Woodcock and was amazed how much he had missed by sleeping soundly in the twilight hours. He didn't realise that the Woodcock had a plumage as cryptic as that of the Nightjar with its subtle browns and patterns which made it almost invisible on the leaf-strewn woodland floor. The Woodcock's ability to see almost 360 degrees at once, ensures he is perfectly-adapted to life on the ground.

As the true darkness set in, the Stonechat decided he needed some sleep to be ready and alert for the following day. The Nightjar swooped across the heather in pursuit of moths as the black cloak of night prevailed.

Other late arrivals include the dashing Hobby whose favourite item on the menu is dragonflies which he hunts on his scythe-like wings, picking them off as they fly across the boggy areas. They usually set up home in a conifer on the edge of the heathlands spending most of the day looking for large flying insects.

Hobby

Soot, the Blackbird was foraging on the ground in a copse on the edge of the heath when he was startled by a large raptor with long-fingered wings alighting on the ground not far away. He thought it unusual as the bird had not dived on an item of prey, and the bird was looking around intently as if he had lost something.

"Lost anything?" Soot enquired helpfully.

The bird turned his head and looked at him with his vivid yellow eyes.

"No, actually, I have found something and that is going to keep me busy," replied the large, mottled, grey-headed bird. He was the size of a Buzzard, but something was different about him.

"You are not a Buzzard, are you? I can see from your eyes and your strange behaviour that there is something different about you," said Soot, confident that his eyes were not playing tricks.

"You are correct. I am not a true Buzzard although they call me a Honey Buzzard—I am a different kettle of fish."

"Why do you say that? You have a similar build, but your tail is longer and your head appears to be much smaller than the average Buzzard."

"You are very observant, I must say," he muttered surprisingly.

Soot blushed with pride that someone had at last recognised his talent. "You said you have found something. I can see no mouse or rabbit so what have you found?"

"Listen!"

The woodland was full of singing birds but that is not what the raptor was referring to. Austin concentrated hard and realised that there was a constant buzzing of bees.

"I can only hear insects but surely that cannot be sufficient for such a big bird as yourself, can it?"

Honey Buzzard

"Actually, that is exactly what I am looking for. I live mainly on insects, especially bees and wasps."

"Well knock me down with a feather! Don't they sting you?"

"Of course, they try but, if you look carefully, I have tightly packed feathers around my face and usually they cannot penetrate this defence," replied the Buzzard in a relieved voice.

"How do you catch them?"

"I don't. I dig up their hives and take their honeycombs to feed the larvae to my chicks. There is a lot of protein in a grub, you know. If you care to take a look at my feet you will see I have thick, stubby talons unlike other hunting birds. They are specialised for digging, not sharp and long like all the other predators. I do often catch a frog or snake when I am wandering around on the ground, but I am not a hunter in the true sense of the word," explained the Honey Buzzard.

"But if you dig up the nests, then the insects will disappear, won't they?"

"If I totally destroyed the nest, then that may be so, but I only take a few honeycombs and leave the rest alone. The bees or wasps will then rebuild their nest. A week or so later, I return to do the same again! I know the location of so many subterranean hives that I am not short of options, you see. I live here in the south of the country where the weather is a little better, and there are more active nests. I also avoid areas of clay as the ground is too heavy to work; these sandy areas are perfect for my family and me."

"How do you find the nests?" Soot was obviously fascinated by this rather peculiar bird.

"Well, I often sail over the trees on my flat wings and just watch which way the bees and wasps are heading. They all return to the nest sometime during the day, so I just have to be patient, eventually, they will show me exactly where they live. On other occasions, I just sit in a tree and watch what is going on. As I said, I am not a dynamic predator, but I do not have to be as my prey is located in one specific place. It's quite simple. However, if the weather is dreadful, then the bee and wasp numbers are much lower and that makes my life much more difficult," replied the Buzzard.

"What do you do in winter when there are no insects about?"

"Well, I am not here! I leave in the autumn and head southwards to Africa. I do not like flying over the open ocean, as there are not many thermals, so I fly over the Straits of

Gibraltar to avoid any problems. My biggest feat* is crossing the Channel to get here!"

"You really are an original bird. I have never heard anything like it. Such a large bird who is solely dependent on insects, it's amazing!"

"Well, you had better stand back as I am going to excavate this wasps' nest. They do get rather agitated, and they may attack you! I thought it fair to give you that warning."

"Thanks! I'll leave you to your digging. Thank you for your most enlightening conversation. Good luck."

"You too," and with that, the Honey Buzzard started digging into the sandy soil, surrounded by a swarm of angry insects.

As autumn approaches Georgie and Pebble witness the departure of the Hobby, Honey Buzzard, Nightjar and the Warblers who migrate southwards, the Curlews move to the coastal estuaries, leaving them to face another winter alone. The reptiles go underground to hibernate to avoid the freezing conditions. The reappearance of the Great Grey Shrike and Winter Thrushes is an indication that the year has turned almost full circle.

Great Grey Shrike

A Mother's Grief

In a city hedgerow, a mother Song Thrush sat on her eggs eagerly awaiting their hatching. She felt fairly secure in her beautifully constructed nest, and her husband was always prompt with his waitering services, bringing her a diet of snails and worms. He had stopped his powerful singing the moment they had constructed the nest, as he didn't want to proclaim the presence of their home to the prying eyes of anyone who wished them harm.

One morning, Bara, the Song Thrush, realised there was slight movement below her. Her brood patch, an area of exposed skin on her lower breast, almost devoid of feathers and full of blood vessels, ensured that she could transfer her body heat to the eggs, picked up a vibration. She stood up to peer down into the gloom of the nest cup. A little white object was protruding from one of the eggs. She knew it was the egg tooth of her first hatchling. This special adaption to the young bird's beak helps it break through the egg shell and assists it in its liberation from its calcium prison; it would disappear a few days later. She watched with fascination as the egg cracked and the little pink, almost embryonic, creature appeared and took its first breath of air. Although appearing extremely unappealing to us, with its bulging closed eyes, wrinkled reptilian* skin and stunted limbs, she was overjoyed that her patient wait had been rewarded.

Once the little fledgling managed to extricate* himself from the shell, the male bird fluttered in and took the blue, spotted egg away and dropped it some distance from the nest site to ensure that there were no obvious clues to the whereabouts of his new family. Over the next few days, he would repeat this operation until there were just four naked chicks sitting in the moss-filled cup.

Each chick showed his character even at this early stage, one more aggressive, the others passive despite being completely blind and naked. Bara, who spent the whole time with them, began to recognise her brood. She would ensure that each would be fed, even the smallest and youngest. Her husband kept up a running commentary, telling her about the availability of food, so she knew that there would be enough to go around. After a few days, they began to open their eyes, and some primitive feathers began to appear. Most of the time, the little birds would expose their brightly-coloured gapes to ensure Bara knew that they were still hungry. Her poor husband was having to do overtime, bringing in food as quickly as possible.

Slowly, but surely, these tiny creatures began to change into little birds rather than the alien-like beings which had emerged from the eggs. Bara's bond grew by the day, and she was as proud as any mother would be. Once the fledglings had acquired their downy feathers, she knew that she could join her husband on the endless task of providing food. She was always aware that there would be dangers in leaving her brood unattended, but the sheer demand for nourishment meant that she had no choice in the matter.

After a few days, she returned to her nest, but something was different. Normally, the rustling of the branches by either her or her husband would stimulate the little birds to *cheep* enthusiastically to be fed. However, there was a deafening silence as she approached the nest. Her heart stopped, a lump appeared in her throat, and an indescribable pain raced through her body. To her horror, the nest was deserted, and her beloved brood gone. She let out an anguished scream which immediately alerted her husband.

"Look! We have been robbed!" she shrieked in despair. "My darling brood extinguished. All our hopes dashed. Those weeks of hard work destroyed within an instant; why is life so cruel?" she sobbed.

Her husband stood silently by, unable to utter any words to express his sheer devastation, unable to console his distraught partner—his tears welling up in his dark eyes.

"Something has taken away my lovely children, and I am inconsolable. Who could perform such an evil deed? They should be ashamed of the pain and suffering they have brought down upon us!" she exclaimed.

A crow, sitting on a branch nearby, looked with a menacing glint in his cold eyes; at least his chicks had had a good meal that day. Nature is harsh, and the victims have to cope with loss fairly frequently, it's just part of the unyielding natural world.

Carrion Crow

Urban Utterances Revisited

A House Sparrow was 'chipping and chirping' merrily on a wall when he was joined by a secretive Dunnock.

"How are you today?" Till the Dunnock asked.

"Not bad, yourself?" replied Chipper the Sparrow.

"Must not grumble, I suppose. I am sitting here watching my partner to make sure she's fine."

"Why shouldn't she be fine?"

"Well, I have built a nest, and I hope she will lay some eggs soon, but there is another male bird hopping about, and I am not sure about his intentions. There are some really sneaky birds around, and I have been told that over 50% of the chicks produced are fathered by another bird!"

"Wow! That's worrying. I can see why you are paying attention! I would be distraught if I thought I was working tirelessly for someone else's kids." Chipper exclaimed.

"Is it me or are your species in decline?" asked Till.

House Sparrow

"You have noticed too, have you? Yes, we are in trouble; our numbers have crashed. Many people think there is a correlation* between the introduction of lead-free petrol, but there could be another factor. There is obviously some kind of air pollutant that is affecting us. Hopefully, when man eventually finds what it is, then they can take steps to solve this problem for us. It is not only this country which is experiencing this problem: every major European city has lost 50 % to 90% of its Sparrow population, so you can see it is a major problem," announced Chipper somewhat downcast.

"That is dreadful news. I hope someone finds out what is causing this catastrophic decline for your species. We also have a few problems here too," remarked Till.

"Why?"

"Obviously, cats are a major problem, but Crows and Magpies are becoming increasingly common, and they love raiding nests, and I have experienced that myself a few times. They are extremely cunning: they sit up in a tree and just spy on the whole neighbourhood, making a mental note of everything they see. They wait patiently, knowing when the eggs are laid or how old the chicks are, and then suddenly, they appear, and all that laborious work was in vain!

"The grey squirrels are also a scourge*; they are as bad as the crows! You are safe in your roof spaces but the birds that nest in the hedges have this to contend with on a daily basis. It's all very disheartening."

"Yes, I can imagine that. I do notice these things myself, and I am grateful that I don't have your problems. By the way, I think your partner has gone into the next garden," Chipper announced.

"Really! I'd better go."

In the hedgerow, a hen Blackbird was sitting quietly on her nest, awaiting the arrival of her new family. She could see through the leaves the busy comings and goings of a Great Tit who was returning to a nearby nest box every few minutes. His beak was invariably full of caterpillars and then she could hear the excitable hubbub of the chicks inside. He had started nesting a little earlier than she had done, and she knew that it wouldn't be long before she and her husband would be out searching for food for her offspring but, at the moment, she could sit in silence and just watch the world go by. She was well aware that there were cats in the area and that both Carrion Crows and Magpies were always on the lookout for unattended eggs or chicks. She knew that only by the dedication and perseverance of her partner and herself would they succeed in their wish to get their young fledged.

A large Wood Pigeon was sitting in a tree when he was joined by a sleek pinkish, grey Dove who alighted with a soft cooing.

"Morning to you," he said. "Busy?"

"No, not really. The wife is sitting on eggs, and it won't be long before the squabs* are in the nest, and then I shall have the unenviable task of being the sole provider; they really do need a lot of feeding you know," replied the Wood Pigeon. "How about you?"

"Same thing really. I am waiting for the eggs to hatch."

"Is it me, or are there more of you around nowadays?"

"Yes, we are doing very well, and we are spreading all the time," replied Twigs, the Collared Dove.

"Spreading, what do you mean by that?"

"Well, it seems like we have been here for ever, but that just isn't the case. We first arrived on this island in the late 1950s and have moved into gardens throughout this country and far beyond that as well," Twigs said proudly.

"Where have you come from then?" asked the inquisitive Pigeon.

"Nearly a century ago, we only had a toe-hold in Europe, living in the gardens of Istanbul in Turkey, but since then, our population has exploded. We have spread across the whole of Europe, then across the Atlantic to Iceland and finally into North America!" Twigs said smugly

"That is some expansion! How did you manage that?"

"I suppose we are a true city bird, we find enough to eat, and utilise every opportunity, hence we could breed well and move onto new places. We are the ultimate example of man's positive influence on a species, and we are truly grateful for his help."

"It's good to hear such a heartening story; perhaps the urban gardens may be the salvation for many species if birds learn to adapt and use the benefits of this habitat. I am sure everything will be rosy," answered the Pigeon.

With that, both birds flew off to see how their partners were faring.

Near the sitting Blackbird was the exquisite nest of a Long-tailed Tit. The long tail of the female was protruding out of the hole of this spherical structure. The male was making his way through the hedge and he passed fairly close to the female Blackbird.

"That is a wonderful nest you have there," she said.

"Oh, thanks. It did take some time to build," replied Bubbles, the Long-tailed Tit, rather proudly.

"It looks a bit small to me," she said rather dismissively.

Long-tailed Tit

"It looks that way at the moment, but it has the capacity to expand as the chicks get bigger," Bubbles explained.

"How is that possible?"

"It is built of feathers, moss and spider webs. There are probably over a thousand feathers in the construction and so it is not only cosy but perfect for our needs," he muttered with an air of pride.

"That really is a work of art and it's good to see that you are now here in town," said the Blackbird.

"Yes, life is getting better here, the bushes are growing, the trees are now mature and best of all, there are feeders in many gardens, so the winter is easier here than in the bare woodlands nearby."

"Absolutely. Life in town has become so much easier, and the future here looks just fine."

The Meeting

Word had been spread to birds both far and near
To meet up to have a chat about their greatest fear
Things needed to be said and heard
To allow many to have a final word
About the plight of this uncertain, ailing world
Views had to be shared and various opinions aired
To ensure that their pain and suffering could be spared
By allowing them a voice that could be heard
Something which would give hope to each and every single bird

After chatting to various species, Darcy thought that it might be useful for everyone to have a meeting to discuss their most pressing issues. He asked his friends to spread the word about the time and place. This duly done both far and wide, and many promised to attend. It was decided to have the meeting in a forest glade where there were enough branches and space for a large number of creatures to congregate*.

The day began with the dew glistening on every blade of grass but slowly, the clouds rolled in as the wind began to gather pace. At the allotted time, the assembled masses waited eagerly to hear what was going to happen. The cool breeze meant the early autumnal speckled leaves were rustling softly throughout the clearing and some of the smaller birds huddled together for warmth.

Darcy stood upon a large rock, cleared his throat, and started to talk: "Welcome one and all, it is wonderful to see you all sitting here, I hope for the next few hours you can get on peacefully and not 'snack' on one of your neighbours!" A ripple of laughter went through the throng of animals.

"I have a message from a few who cannot attend: Turpin, the Swift, said he couldn't be present because he can neither stop nor perch! He thought it would be a bit difficult for everyone to concentrate having him zooming over our heads incessantly trying to hear the debate. Darcy turned his head and noticed a few Swallows sitting on the narrowest of branches. Perhaps one of you would be kind enough to pass on the main points of our meeting to him." They nodded their heads to acknowledge his request.

"I have heard so many stories, but I think it would be useful to have a summary of all our problems so that we have some clarity and understanding on the issues we are facing and then, maybe, the message could be passed on to those who can change it. May I suggest that we divide up into groups as we all have our own special needs and problems. Perhaps the best would be four groups: the hunters, the hunted (which also includes me!), the summer migrants and, if there are any left, the winter visitors. Talk amongst yourselves and come up with a brief summary of what is worrying you."

All the birds nodded in agreement—they realised Darcy did have a bit of nous*, and perhaps, something could be achieved from this get-together. "Let's reconvene in a little while and get your feedback," he added, just to make sure that there was some urgency and concentration on the task in hand.

The murmuring started and even some heated discussions broke out —this was the first time the birds had actually spoken to their neighbours and found out so many similarities; they realised that everyone was experiencing the same emotions but the threats differed. Suddenly, there was an understanding between the species and they knew a problem shared might hold the answer.

A few minutes later, after speaking to his group, Darcy flew back onto the rock and addressed the meeting once again. "Ladies and gentlemen, please, may I ask for a spokesman from each group. Let's start with the predators, shall we?" He made a quick dash to clear the 'stage' as a stunning Red Kite swooped down and landed on the rock.

"Well, I know many of you are afraid of us, but we are worried too. We need prey to feed our young and when creatures like you disappear, so do we. We are the barometer of the environment, and when humans realise we are no longer present, it means there are huge underlying problems with our world. They realised that the indiscriminate use of herbicides and pesticides does have a damaging impact on the whole food chain and it's good to know, they are now taking more care with what they spray on their fields. I am sure you are familiar with the story of DDT and the consequences of that evil concoction."

Every single bird nodded in approval.

"There has been an improvement in their attitude towards hunting birds. We were shot and poisoned indiscriminately* a few years ago. My species was down to just a few birds in Wales, but man took an active step to reintroduce us across the country, and, with a healthier environment, we have thrived and spread across most of this island. As you know, I have only been back for a year or so, and I am living proof that when positive and appropriate actions are taken, we have the ability to bounce back."

"That's fantastic!" someone shouted out.

"However, on my travels southwards, I met up with some vultures who told me about some birds who are still suffering from a man-made problem. It seems vets are injecting farm animals with a chemical called 'diclofenac,' which is poisonous to the carrion* eaters, and many Indian vulture species are facing extinction having experienced a 95% crash in their numbers. I hear that some European organisations are pressing to have this chemical banned here, so hopefully, we won't see the eradication of our European vultures. Once they have addressed the problems of illegal shooting and poisoning, we should all thrive once again!

Red Kite

"Unfortunately, some of our kind, especially the Hen Harrier, are still being persecuted—this bird is threatened with extirpation* despite other raptors* doing well. Humans need to help this beautiful creature, or it will disappear from these islands. There is nothing more splendid and enthralling than watching the ghost-like male performing his 'sky dancing' in the spring. I have witnessed this spectacle, and it would be the greatest travesty should this species disappear from our skies. These Harriers are especially targeted on driven Grouse moors and, unless there are much stricter penalties imposed on these estates, they will continue to disappear. Planned wind farms on moorlands should also be considered extremely carefully as they will have a negative impact on these magnificent creatures. Otherwise, things are looking brighter for us than they have for years, and long may it continue. Thank you."

This was followed by a round of applause from the audience who wanted to show their appreciation. The Kite bowed his head magnanimously* and then rose majestically into the air—his forked, cinnamon tail glowing as he glided back to the grassy knoll* to join the Falcons and hawks; he looked around his group, somewhat bashfully.

Knowing that the threat was over, Darcy flew back to the stone and addressed the meeting once again. "Thank you, Mr

Kite, very succinctly* said, we are pleased to know that some of your greatest threats are being addressed. We all hope it persists but naturally, we are still rather anxious of you and your kind. Who would like to have their say?" he enquired whilst looking around for a volunteer.

Romer a brightly coloured Redstart alighted next to him. He looked wonderful with his splendid, water-coloured tangerine breast, black throat, contrasting with his white forecrown and grey nape and back—a truly resplendent Chat.

Redstart

He nodded to Darcy, "I would like to say a few words about the migratory species, of which I am one. We have the daunting task of flying thousands of miles each year to survive. Most migratory birds have a dreadful mortality rate with over 50% of the youngsters not surviving their first trip. We crave the warmth of summer, which provides us with the plentiful insect life we need. We fly here not only for the food source but also for the 20 hours of daylight at this time of year which ensures we have enough opportunities to provide sufficient nourishment for our offspring. If the day length did not change, we would not contemplate this hazardous and tiring journey every year."

"Hear! Hear!" the rest of the migrants cried out. "Tell them about our problems!"

"Well, I was coming to that. We are threatened on our huge journeys by predators such as Hobbies, and the squadrons of Eleonora's Falcons who breed on some Mediterranean islands. This species even delays its breeding season until the autumn when they know there will be a multitude of small birds heading south to escape the freezing northern climes. Yet, their threat is nothing compared to the evil activities of man in the Mediterranean whose hunting means a million deaths a day!

"What chance do we have against lime sticks, mist nets, traps and the gun! Nearly every migratory species has been decimated by their inhumane and heartless activities." He cast his eyes downwards to hide the grief that was welling up inside him.

A few sobs could be heard from the others especially those who endured this danger every time they migrated.

"Unless something is done, we face a future full of trepidation.* Not only that, the desertification* of Southern Europe and mid-Africa is making our winter quarters less appealing. Goats are destroying the bushes we need, and water is becoming rare. Even the seasons are changing here on our breeding grounds: spring is arriving earlier, and for this reason, we have to follow this trend. This means moving northwards sooner than we used to. How can these factors be addressed? None of us have the answers, but it weighs heavily upon us all. I have had my say." He then flitted across the glade and sat on a branch, his red tail shimmering as he did so.

"Thank you, my friend," said Darcy. "Well, you have heard from two groups: one fairly encouraging, whereas the other is extremely worrying. Who's next? How about a resident? I don't want to hog the conversation, so any volunteers?"

A Robin hopped confidently onto the roughly-hewn rock and began to address the participants.

"Friends, enemies, I am extremely humbled to be able to have my say. I cannot grumble about life here in this pristine, verdant valley—it seems that whoever is responsible is extremely sympathetic to our needs. Very little has changed here, and so we have been able to succeed without too much trouble. However, away from here, our habitats are being destroyed by constant human developments: new houses, new roads, more farmland, the constant noise depriving us of our quiet places. Farmers are still tearing up hedges, so many birds have nowhere to nest.

"The new chemicals they use are poisoning bees and, without their busy pollen collecting, there will be no fruits or seeds, which will wipe out life as we know it. Pollution to the air and water has led to local extinctions of certain species and there seems little that can be done about it.

"Other problems have been caused by the introduction of non-indigenous animals and plants. Our nests are at risk from mink, fresh water invertebrates are being eradicated by the American crayfish, and our local crayfish are quickly disappearing from our rivers. The Red Squirrel has been annihilated* by the American Grey Squirrel who is not only more aggressive, but also carries squirrel-pox, a deadly virus to our native species. It only takes one grey squirrel to infect a local population causing fatal consequences. Our native squirrel has retreated from the southern counties and is now only found in the more unfavourable areas of Scotland and Wales. This is an enormous tragedy and a result of pure ignorance; why do they think they can introduce new animals without considering the dire consequences of their deeds?

"Notwithstanding, I have to admit that there are many positives in the urban areas; the gardens and the provision of food by people have allowed so many species to venture into town to set up home. Many are thriving and hopefully, that will encourage others to create wildlife gardens allowing even more animals to use this habitat. In this respect, humans have made a valuable contribution to maintaining numbers. I think that's about it. I would like to express my gratitude for your attentiveness."

All the birds clapped and cheered as the Robin made his way back to his group.

Darcy assumed his place on the 'talking rock' "Thank you, Mr Robin, a mixed tale for the creatures who do not stray very far from their birthplace. I have such special needs that perhaps I have not been aware of the problems facing creatures away from the river," he admitted whilst shuffling around somewhat uncomfortably. He continued by asking, "Do we have any winter visitors here? I know it's late in the season but has anyone remained or has returned early?"

A Redwing fluttered down to the rock and looked out over the crowded glade. His russet sides and yellow eyebrows made him look almost exotic.

Redwing

"You are correct in your assumption, Mr Dipper, all the Winter Thrushes returned to mainland Europe in spring, but I hurt my wing just before I was due to fly northwards and so I remained, hoping my injuries would heal; luckily, they have. As a winter visitor, I have a very different opinion to this land. Many seem to have realised that it is a wonderful experience having wildlife in their gardens and many fruit trees have been planted especially for us. Crab apple trees, cotoneaster, rowan have never been more common, and so Winter Thrushes do have a harvest; things are much better than before.

"Food and fresh water is now being provided in many gardens, and we really do benefit from this change in attitude. However, our biggest threat is the cat. They are ruthless and canny hunters. Millions of birds of various species meet their deaths at the claws of this skilful 'pet'. If only the owners could keep them indoors or at least put a bell around their necks! Then we would be aware of the danger hiding under a bush or hidden within a hedgerow."

"Absolutely!" was the reaction from all the birds.

"Not only that, but there are great changes, both here and at home. We have experienced another mild winter, if this trend continues, then I see no point in migrating across that rough, dark sea in the autumn as we are at risk to the vagaries of this fickle climate!"

A murmur of agreement was shared by everyone. They had all experienced the changeable weather for themselves, when a sudden, almost imperceptible, gust of wind made the leaves rustle once again.

"My tundra homeland is changing too," he continued. "The plants and insects are having to adapt to the ameliorating climate. We have to move farther northwards or ascend into the mountains to find the right habitat. We have resident birds who do not migrate. The Ptarmigan is an excellent example; this Arctic-loving Grouse has very specialised needs, but its surroundings are evolving to its detriment. They cannot survive the warming of the climate, they will have to move farther north, and will be sorely missed from my home territory. It is clear that the more specialised you are, the more you are under threat from any minimal shift in the weather or temperature. The 'specialists' face a bleak and uncertain future, I am afraid. I think I have covered the main points and, on that note, I shall hand over to the next speaker."

"Well done, Mr Redwing. Some sobering thoughts there. How about a view from a pelagic* species?" Darcy asked looking towards the seabirds.

A Guillemot was elected to be the spokesperson for the cliff dwellers. He landed clumsily on the 'talking rock'. Unlike most birds, he could not stand upright but sat on his lower legs, his webbed feet looking rather comical as they splayed over the edge of the boulder. He looked a little embarrassed at his awkwardness. "Sorry about the entrance, but my wings aren't the best! They are basically paddles for flying underwater, where they are the perfect adornment. Well, what shall I say?

"I am here to represent the seabird colonies and put you in the picture of how we are coping. The cliffs have been there since time immemorial, and I am sure they will be in centuries to come. Whether we will be, is questionable! The seas are changing, and certain fish are becoming rarer which threatens our existence: without this rich resource, we cannot stay where we are. Over-fishing near our breeding grounds has had a very adverse effect on our breeding success. Perhaps the colder seas to the north may provide the solution, but who knows the answer to that question?

"There have been a number of catastrophic accidents involving oil-laden vessels*, and the resultant pollution has killed many thousands of birds. If man can keep his oil to himself and not spread it across the oceans, we would certainly all be very grateful. The amount of plastics floating in the seas is an extremely worrying development. Thousands are choking to death by ingesting rubbish thrown into the sea. Youngsters have their gullets crammed full of discarded plastics and die in the most painful and repugnant way. Remote islands are littered with rubbish, metres deep, originating from thousands of miles away. I really do not know what to suggest but this issue has to be addressed immediately," he explained almost tearfully. He took a large gulp of air and managed to continue.

Utter silence was the response.

"Finally, our breeding grounds need to be protected from rodents as they steal our eggs or kill our young. I know many islands have been improved by eradicating rodents and hedgehogs. I hope these measures continue. Man has acknowledged his impact and he is trying hard to preserve the rarest of creatures. Perhaps, we shall all be offered this protection eventually and our breeding success will improve too. I think I have covered the main points. Thank you once more for your patience."

With whirring wings, the Guillemot managed to get airborne and went back to his cliff-loving friends. A round of applause from the audience was given, and a few tears were wiped away from some moistened eyes.

"Anyone else?" asked Darcy after a brief pause.

Chester, the Curlew, flew onto the rock and bowed to the enraptured* masses.

"Thank you for giving me the opportunity to address you. I am here to represent the birds from the estuaries. This habitat is forever changing with the interaction between the sea, the shore and a river; it is such an important biotope*. It provides a refuge for so many species and provides such a rich source of food. It is a vital stopping off point for migrants passing through on their long journeys, as well as birds who remain here to breed. In this country, there are many positives: the breeding areas are often protected by special fences to prevent rodents from getting to the ground-nesting birds. This has allowed some species to thrive which is a heartening trend.

"However, the situation in other countries is not so good. Some of the estuaries are being adversely affected by the development of tourist centres. One of the most important wetland areas in Spain is being sucked dry by the over extraction of water by farmers, tourists and residents. It's a catastrophe in the making. The sole reason that many people visit that area is for the wildlife, yet, it is disappearing before their very eyes! I just hope man learns from his mistakes before it's too late. We cannot afford to lose such precious and irreplaceable habitats. That's all I have to add."

With that, Chester flapped his wings and flew back to his friends siting nearby.

"I would like to thank all the speakers for giving us your stories. There seems to be a common thread to them all. Where people are more aware of the benefits of having a healthy environment, we seem to be doing fairly well. Hopefully, when new chemicals are developed, man will not want to repeat the follies*of the past.

"In some countries, we are hunted mercilessly for profit, —why isn't more pressure being put upon these nations from the more 'enlightened'? I shall never know. I feel that

Man is more aware of his negative influence on the planet and they are beginning to realise they need us around as we are the true indicators of the health of the world. Where positive steps are taken, we bounce back and that is encouraging for all.

"I believe that things have improved here; the Victorian attitude of shooting everything and having them stuffed to adorn their houses has, fortunately, changed. The intervention by some brave Victorian women in 1889 to stop the slaughter of many beautiful birds for their fine plumes was the catalyst* for change; from that moment, things have looked more promising. The evil, common practice of egg collecting which was so prevalent* in the past has been reduced. There are far fewer fools left carrying out this dreadful deed."

"Thank goodness for that!" someone shouted out. The others chuckled in agreement.

"It seems that once people become more interested and knowledgeable in the natural world, they do try to make the right decisions, and that is commendable. They have taken active steps to reintroduce or relocate species such as the successful projects with the White-tailed Eagle, Red Kite, Osprey, Crane and Corncrake. There are even plans afoot to bring back the White Stork which disappeared as a breeding bird over 500 years ago! They are now trying to make amends for the extinctions they brought about and are considering bringing back the beaver and the super predators such as the wolf and even the lynx! This would bring the food chain back into a natural equilibrium*.

"Nevertheless, I fear that one day, humans may wake up to a deafening silence and only then, will they realise what is missing from their lives. The spring melodies will become just a memory for some and an unfulfilled experience for those to come." He paused to reflect on the gravity of what he had said and then continued in a rather sullen* voice.

Many species around the world have disappeared for ever and now some of our European birds are facing the same fate.

Turtle Dove

"This has already begun with the *purring* of the Turtle Dove becoming a rarity for many, with a 90% drop in its population in the last 20 years or so, a truly catastrophic consequence of hunting, ignorance, greed and disinterest. The sands of time are running out for many of us and the impending silence may be the only motivation for change.

Our wildlife sanctuaries need protection and more should be established to shelter the silent, the weak and the vulnerable. I ask, is this just a dream or will ambivalence and self-interest prevail?

"I have heard that there are international laws to protect us but why are we still being hunted indiscriminately?"

"That's a good question! Will it ever change?" someone screamed out.

"Perhaps, if they realise how many of us are facing extinction and that one million of us are killed each day in Europe alone; then a movement to ban the annual massacre of songbirds might come into effect. They need to look deeply into their souls and analyse what is truly important in their lives. The natural world is something to be cherished.

"This unique, complex and stunning planet is here to be shared by all and the beautiful and fascinating creatures have every right to be left in peace. Mankind must learn not to be self-absorbed. He must respect the Earth and show understanding and consideration to every living being on this planet. Every extinct species depletes this place of an interesting and irreplaceable life form. Man listens to our pleasing songs, but they do not hear our pleading voices. We have the right to be here and to be heard."

The birds looked at each other and nodded. These profound words had touched the depths of their very being. Their hearts were torn asunder but they were confident that Darcy would reach a well-reasoned and optimistic conclusion. They trusted his wisdom and so they asked.

"How can we be heard? What can be done?"

There was a definite surge in optimism as his words resonated* among the assembled creatures. His calming sentiments had allayed* their darkest fears, his analytical approach was enlightening. Even now the weather seemed to respond when a beam of sunshine suddenly lit up the whole glade bringing warmth to what had been a rather chilly morn.

"Well, I believe that everyone needs to be informed," Darcy answered authoritatively.

"How and when?" came the unanimous response.

"We need to get the message out to the younger generations—they will be the decision-makers of the future. If they inherit an interest in the natural world, I truly believe they have the potential to help us. Their awareness could bring about beneficial changes for us all."

"How can we tell them our stories?" they asked expectantly.

He scratched his head, puffed up his chest, and then proclaimed in a very calm, thoughtful and reassuring way.

"We already have."

Postscript

Each year, I eagerly await the excited screaming of the Swifts. Their evocative calls have been imprinted in my very soul from a very young age. I could never envisage a summer without them and once their calls disappear in late July, a deep sense of melancholy weighs down upon me, as I know another nine months of darkness, cold and emptiness will have to pass before their scythe-shaped forms will cut the skies, accompanied by their screeching. They are the true harbingers of the ardent season.

Some time has passed since I completed the book but it seems that Darcy's prophetic warnings of the silence descending upon man has already begun. My beloved Swifts have not returned to my local colony this spring, my joy at hearing their screams crushed by their absence. I never, imagined that this would occur in my lifetime. Who knows what other songs will soon be just a memory—as the major players in the orchestra forsake our lands, the symphony will sound tinny and their moving and magical stanzas will be greatly missed.

I am overwhelmed by their loss and my fear grows year-on-year as certain birds disappear from our countryside. What happened to my local colony of Swifts? I have never experienced their absence and will they ever return? I have another winter to wait to find that answer but it's going to be a long time, full of consternation.

Explanation

The title of the book is a derivation from the saying 'from the horse's mouth': from the original source. The stories are based on fact and, therefore, it's a fitting title. The cover design boldly portrays the problems facing birds and the marionettes depict that birds have no power at all to change their destiny—we totally control their lives both directly and indirectly.

Fox Cubs

What Can I Do to Help? A Few Hints

If you have a garden, make a bird bath from an upturned dustbin lid. Make sure it does not freeze in the winter, but do not add anything to keep it ice free. Put out bird feeders to encourage wildlife into your garden, but do not forget to keep them clean as mouldy nuts and seeds are poisonous!

Put up a nest box but make sure it is not facing south as it will be too hot in the summer. Perhaps a bat box could be erected to encourage these fascinating mammals into your garden.

If there is a compost heap in the garden, be careful when it is being emptied as there may be slow worms or even a hedgehog living inside. Have a pile of logs in one corner with a space inside; a hedgehog may hibernate there during the winter. In autumn, check that your bonfire is empty before you set it alight! Don't forget that hedgehogs cannot have milk so leave out some water and perhaps a bowl of dog or cat food. There are even special foods which can be bought from some pet stores.

You can make an insect hotel by tying a bundle of canes together. Solitary bees and wasps will lay their eggs there.

Leave one area of the garden 'wild', or plant meadow grass which will encourage butterflies and other insects.

Best of all, build a pond with a sloping side which will allow birds and animals to drink. Amphibians and dragonflies will usually find their own way into this new sanctuary.

Join the RSPB or a local conservation society. Keep a wildlife diary and record your observations—they may, one day, show you how much the wildlife in your garden has changed. Try to encourage others to follow your actions. The animals and birds will be eternally grateful.

Thank you so much.

Glossary

Urban Utterances
Leatherjacket	Pupae of a Crane fly
Rifled	Raided

The River and an Unusual Visitor
Dank	Unpleasantly cold and damp
Gnarled	Knobbly and twisted
Enigmatic	Mysterious
Aurora Borealis	An incredible electrical phenomenon where there is an interaction between atoms in the Arctic air and the sun's rays which produces a huge array of moving colours in the night sky.
Pillage	To steal everything
Sardonic	In a mocking way
Fjord	A steep sided valley joining the sea in Norway
Tang	Taste
Invertebrates	Animals without a backbone
Recluse	A person who keeps away from other people
Biosphere	Environment
Parrying	Defending yourself when attacked
Tor	A granite structure on the top of some moorlands especially on Dartmoor and Bodmin Moor.
Demise	Death
Insatiable	Cannot be satisfied
Voracious	Greedy
Nefarious	Evil
Dapper	Smart
Usurper	Someone trying to take control
Scree	Broken rocks at the base of a cliff
Vociferous	Most vocal
Plaintive	Sad, melancholic sound

Stanza	A collection of musical notes
Copse	Small wood

Spring Arrives

Myriad	Countless, infinite
Onomatopoeic	A word that mimics the sound of something
Noxious	Poisonous
Avian	Relating to birds
Amelioration	Improvement
Desertification	The process of areas becoming more arid and finally becoming a desert.
Mist net	A fine mesh net which is virtually invisible
Metamorphosis	Change
Verdant	Green
Travails	Difficulties
Incredulously	In an unbelieving manner
Piebald	Black and white
Frenetic	At a very fast pace
Quarry	Prey
Waning	Disappearing, diminishing

Family Life

Wistfully	With a feeling of regretful longing

The Wheatear and the Peregrine

Moustachial	Like a moustache
Panacea	Solution or remedy
Ramifications	The unwelcome consequences
Ornithology	The study of birds
Dissipated	Vanished
Haunts	Homes or territories
Adept	Better at doing something
Evolution	The process how a species adapts to its environment
Honing	Improving or perfecting

The Pigeon and the Cuckoo

Nefarious	Evil

High Fliers

Banshee   A wailing female spirit of Irish legends
Unscathed   Without damage or injury
Fickle   Very changeable

Autumn Approaches

Spangled   Of various colours
Forsake   Leave (forsake, forsook, forsaken)
Discarded   Get rid of
Remorselessly Heartlessly, ruthlessly
Cacophony   Deafening noise
Cache   Store of food

Cliff Hangers

Vying   Fighting for
Marauding   Looking to kill or steal
Guano   Bird poo
Evocative   Something that reminds you of something else
Flotsam and jetsam Things which float or have been thrown away into the sea
Strata   Layers
Desalinate   Take salt away
Pelagic   Relating to the sea
Apocalypse   The end of the world
Sagaciously   In a wise way
Concoction   Mixture

Estuary Echoes

Plethora   Abundance
Dapper   Smart
Palpable   Could be felt
Diminutive   Small
Puny   Small and insignificant
Ice Floes   Floating ice
Inevitable   Cannot be avoided
Faring   Performing
Millinery   Hat making
Surreptitious Sly, sneaky, secretive

Reed-bed Ramblings

Reverberate	Echo
Emanate	Coming from
Crepuscular	Relating to the twilight hours

Moorland Muses

Mournful	Extremely sad
Endemic	Species only found in one place
Quarry	Target species, prey
Unscrupulous	Without any morals
Reverberating	Echoing
Lek	Displaying area for some species
Feigning	Pretending

Northern Lights

Machair	Coastal estuarine grasslands
Lochan	Small lake
Suitors	A prospective husband
Ungainly	Awkward in movement
Livery	Uniform, outfit, costume
Regal	Royal
Retiring	Shy
Crofters	Farmers of small Scottish properties
Rump	Small remnant
Indictment	Serving as an illustration that something is wrong.
Reclusive	Keeping away from people

Heathland Haunts

Tardy	Late
Indigenous	Native to an area
Crepuscular	Relating to the twilight
Symbiotic	A positive relationship between two different species
Cryptic	Mysterious and obscure
Idiosyncratic	Unique
Feat	Achievement

A Mother' Grief

Reptilian	Like a reptile

Extricate	Escape from
Correlation	A link

Urban Utterances Revisited

Squab	Baby pigeon
Scourge	Menace or evil

The Meeting

Congregate	Assemble together
Nous	Common sense (pronounced like house)
Transient	Passing through
Succinctly	Said in a clear, short way
Annihilated	Destroyed
Extirpated	Eradicated
Raptors	Birds of prey
Trepidation	Great fear
Biotope	Habitat, environment
Follies	Mistakes
Indiscriminately	Randomly without reason
Carrion	Dead animals/birds
Knoll	Small hill
Magnanimously	In a generous or forgiving way
Enraptured	Entranced, spell-bound, fascinated
Ameliorating	Improving
Oil laden vessels	Ships carrying crude oil
Equilibrium	Balance
Throng	Group, crowd
Prevalent	Common
Catalyst	The 'spark' that causes a change
Equilibrium	Balance
Sullen	Sad
Allayed	Reduced
Resonated	Echoed

List of Plates and Photographs

List of Species Mentioned

Dipper	*Cinclus cinclus*
Great Crested Grebe	*Podiceps cristatus*
Fulmar	*Fulmarus glacialis*
Shag	*Phalacrocorax aristotelis*
Gannet	*Sula bassanus*
Manx Shearwater	*Puffinus puffinus*
Little Egret	*Egretta garzetta*
Grey Heron	*Ardea cinerea*
White Stork	*Ciconia ciconia*
Whooper Swan	*Cygnus cygnus*
Brent Goose	*Branta bernicla*
Osprey	*Pandion haliaetus*
Sparrowhawk	*Accipiter nisus*
Goshawk	*Accipiter gentilis*
Red Kite	*Milvus milvus*
Hen Harrier	*Circus cyaneus*
Marsh Harrier	*Circus aeruginosus*
Buzzard	*Buteo buteo*
Honey Buzzard	*Pernis apivorus*
Golden Eagle	*Aquila chrysaetos.*
White-tailed Eagle	*Haliaeetus albicilla*
Peregrine Falcon	*Falco peregrinus*
Gyr Falcon	*Falco rusticolus*
Kestrel	*Falco tinnunculus*
Merlin	*Falco columbarius*
Hobby	*Falco subbuteo*
Eleanora's Falcon	*Falco eleanorae*
Black Grouse	*Tetrao tetrix*
Red Grouse	*Lagopus lagopus*
Ptarmigan	*Lagopus muta*
Pheasant	*Phasianus colchicus*

Sanderling	*Calidris alba*
Purple Sandpiper	*Calidris maritima*
Golden Plover	*Pluvialis apricaria*
Redshank	*Tringa totanus*
Ruff	*Philomachus pugnax*
Snipe	*Gallinago gallinago*
Woodcock	*Scolopax rusticola*
Bar-tailed Godwit	*Limosa lapponica*
Curlew	*Numenius arquata*
Common Sandpiper	*Actitis hypoleucos*
Red necked Phalarope	*Phalaropus lobatus*
Corncrake	*Crex crex*
Arctic Skua	*Stercorarius parasiticus*
Great Skua	*Catharacta skua*
Mediterranean Gull	*Larus melanocephalus*
Black headed Gull	*Larus ridibundus*
Herring Gull	*Larus argentatus*
Great Black-backed Gull	*Larus marinus*
Common Gull	*Larus canus*
Kittiwake	*Rissa tridactyla*
Sandwich Tern	*Sterna sandvicensis*
Common Tern	*Sterna hirundo*
Arctic Tern	*Sterna paradisaea*
Little Tern	*Sterna albifrons*
Razorbill	*Alca torda*
Guillemot	*Uria aalge*
Puffin	*Fratercula arctica*
Collared Dove	*Streptopelia decaocto*
Wood Pigeon	*Columba palumbus*
Woodlark	*Lullula arborea*
Skylark	*Alauda arvensis*
Barn Swallow	*Hirundo rustica*

House Martin	*Delichon urbica*
Sand Martin	*Riparia riparia*
Tree Pipit	*Anthus trivialis*
Meadow Pipit	*Anthus pratensis*
Barn Owl	*Tyto alba*
Nightjar	*Caprimulgus europaeous*
Pied Wagtail	*Motacilla alba*
Grey Wagtail	*Motacilla cinerea*
Wren	*Troglodytes troglodytes*
Robin	*Erithacus rubecula*
Stonechat	*Saxicola torquata*
Wheatear	*Oenanthe oenanthe*
Whinchat	*Saxicola rubetra*
Redstart	*Phoenicurus phoenicurus*
Ring Ouzel	*Turdus torquatus*
Blackbird	*Turdus merula*
Song Thrush	*Turdus philomelos*
Fieldfare	*Turdus pilaris*
Redwing	*Turdus iliacus*
Sedge Warbler	*Acrocephalus shoenobaenus*
Reed Warbler	*Acrocephalus scirpaceus*
Cettís Warbler	*Cettia cetti*
Dartford Warbler	*Sylvia undata*
Blackcap	*Sylvia atricapilla*
Chiffchaff	*Phylloscopus collybita*
Willow Warbler	*Phylloscopus trochilus*
Goldcrest	*Regulus regulus*
Swift	*Apus apus*
Pied Flycatcher	*Ficedula hypoleuca*
Great Grey Shrike	*Lanius excubitor*
Great Tit	*Parus major*
Bearded Tit	*Panurus biarmicus*

Blue Tit	*Parus caeruleus*
Long-tailed Tit	*Aegithalos caudatus*
Starling.	*Sterna vulgaris*
Chaffinch	*Fringilla coelebs*
Linnet	*Carduelis cannabina*
Greenfinch	*Carduelis carduelis*
Goldfinch	*Carduelis carduelis*
House Sparrow	*Passer domesticas*
Dunnock (Hedge Sparrow)	*Prunella modularis*
Waxwing	*Bombycilla garrulous*
Raven	*Corvus corax*
Carrion Crow	*Corvus corone*
Jay	*Garrulus glandarius*
Magpie	*Pica pica*

Sparrowhawk

Readers' Reviews

"A lovely production and a skilful way of presenting so much information in such an interesting way."
May Whittington (TEFL teacher)

"A fascinating insight into lives of birds accompanied by some lovely photographs and sketches. A book for all ages."
D. Smith (Ornithologist)

"I never knew that so many interesting facts could be crammed into such a small book. The relaxed, informative style swept me along this fascinating non-stop journey of discovery."
Paul Atkins (Ecologist)

"A wonderful book. What an absolute joy, the sketches are amazing as are Dorian's photos. I loved the humour, the environmental factors and the strong message it gives to young people."
(F Bourne)

"So much information is packed into this little book; it opened a door into a world I had never considered before."
J Daer (university lecturer)

"A wonderful collection of anecdotes which are so informative. A pleasure to read."
(N. Solly-Flood DOS)